White Magic

White Magic

RUSSIAN ÉMIGRÉ TALES OF MYSTERY AND TERROR

Translated by Muireann Maguire

Illustrations by Asya Lisina

russian life
BOOKS

Cover illustration: Asya Lisina

ISBN 978-1-880100-76-9

Library of Congress Control Number: 2021938752

Russian Life Books
PO Box 567
Montpelier, VT 05601-0567
russianlife.com
orders@russianlife.com
phone 802-223-4955

CONTENTS

ACKNOWLEDGEMENTS

This collection has been almost a decade in the making; the cast of authors has changed many times, and many people have offered encouragement and inspiration. I would like to thank my former professor of Russian at Trinity College Dublin, Justin Doherty, for introducing me to Russian Symbolism and modernism (including Gaito Gazdanov and his taxi), which are at the core of this collection. Justin's translation of Georgy Ivanov's "The Atom Explodes" (1938), published elsewhere, will knock your socks off. I am also grateful to Paul Richardson for keeping faith with this project even when there was no room at the inn in Exeter. Special gratitude is due to Nora Favorov for her close reading of these translations. Nora and her husband Oleg provided an inexhaustible fund of linguistic and toponymic knowledge, kind words, and good humor; Nora has steered me clear of the pit of translation disaster many times, and her garnet necklace is in the post. Thank you also to my family, whom I hope will enjoy these magical mystery tales.

Every effort has been made to trace copyright holders for the original texts translated in this collection. In particular, I would like to thank Anna Golombiovskaya and Agnes Szydlowski for kindly granting permission to use texts by Irina Odoyevtseva and Nadezhda Teffi, respectively; Professor Xenia Muratova for encouraging me to translate the short fiction of her distinguished uncle Pavel Muratov; Anne-Marie Jackson, Bryan Karetnyk and the ever-lovely Boris Dralyuk for assistance in identifying copyright holders; and my

Francophone colleague Adam Horsley, for helping me reach out to several of the latter. A previous version of my translation of "Kum" by Georgy Peskov (Yelena Deisha) appeared in the online literary magazine *Spolia* (Autumn 2013).

TRANSLATOR'S INTRODUCTION

All thirteen tales in this volume – a baker's dozen – were written by Russian émigrés, writers who fled their native country in the early twentieth century to avoid the turmoil of war and revolution. Scholars call this the "first wave" of emigration (there would be four in all by the century's end): it was also the most abrupt and disorienting for those displaced into refugee camps in Turkey and Bulgaria, slums in Prague or Berlin, and even apartments in Harbin or Paris.[1] For the most part, their sympathies lay with the losing side in the October Revolution of 1917 and Russia's subsequent Civil War between the pro-Soviet Red Army and the tsarist White Army. The latter fought unsuccessfully to restore the last tsar, Nicholas II (executed in 1918), and the old imperial order. The conflict wore on bloodily until 1922. Some Russian writers who left Russia in this first wave of flight later gained global recognition (like the novelist Vladimir Nabokov, who needs no introduction, or Ivan Bunin, winner of the Nobel Prize for Literature in 1933, or even the historical novelist Mark Aldanov, widely translated in the mid-twentieth century). Others were known only within the émigré community (like Nadezhda Teffi). The vast majority eked out a meagre living doing menial work for which they were vastly overqualified (famously, Gaito Gazdanov, who spent two decades driving a taxi around Paris). The nine writers represented in these thirteen stories dispersed all over Europe after 1917, settling

---

1. For more on the plight of Russian writers abroad, see Leonid Livak, *How It Was Done in Paris: Russian Émigré Literature and French Modernism* (Madison: University of Wisconsin Press, 2003) and Marc Raeff, *Russia Abroad: A Cultural History of the Russian Emigration, 1919-1939* (New York and Oxford: Oxford University Press, 1990).

temporarily or permanently in Riga, Rome, Berlin, Paris, Hamburg, and, perhaps most exotically of all, a manor house in County Waterford, Ireland (Pavel Muratov). The only one of these nine to return to Russia did so involuntarily, and died there: Pyotr Krasnov, a former White Army general, led a Cossack cavalry division of the Wehrmacht during the Second World War. Forcibly repatriated to the Soviet Union in 1945, he was executed for treason two years later.

With so much tragedy, it's tempting to argue that exile, as a spiritual condition, is inherently spectral. Writing from exile is one of the most evocative and elusive genres in world literature. As, however, Maria Rubins suggests in her study of the Russian diaspora, to picture the Russian émigré author as a mournful, traumatized character is to subscribe to an unnecessarily reductive cliché.[2] Certainly, émigrés were deracinated from their homeland, and estranged from the new societies and cultures they experienced. They surely underwent nostalgia and yearning for Imperial Russia, where all of the writers included in this volume had led relatively privileged lives. But this regret did not prevent them from putting down new roots in foreign communities, like the heroine of Irina Odoyevtseva's "By The Sea." Some, like Krasnov, preserved restorative passion for Old Russia that amounted to "messianism";[3] others, like Ivan Lukash or Gaito Gazdanov, considered themselves heirs to the tradition of Russian literary prose. The earliest of the writers featured in this anthology, Alexander Amfiteatrov, was first sent into exile by Tsar Nicholas II, in 1902; he chose to return to Russia briefly after the Revolution, but soon left again for Italy, finding Soviet censorship as incompatible with his politics as the Tsar's had been.

As different as all nine writers and their experiences of exile may have been, these thirteen stories are united by a single theme:

---

2. Maria Rubins, "The Unbearable Lightness of Being a Diasporian: Modes of Writing and Reading Narratives of Displacement," in Maria Rubins, ed. *Redefining Russian Literary Diaspora, 1920-2020* (London: UCL Press, 2021), pp. 3-34 (p. 8).

3. Bryan Karetnyk, 'Introduction', in Karetnyk (ed.), *Russian Émigré Short Stories from Bunin to Yanovsky* (London: Penguin, 2017), pp. xiii-xviii (p. xxi).

mystery. In the majority of these stories, that mystery is supernatural. In Amfiteatrov's stories, "He" (1893) and "The Cimmerian Disease" (1896), an innocent narrator or frame narrator becomes the unwitting victim of a vampire-like creature that rapidly destroys their mental and physical health. The plot of "The Cimmerian Disease" appears, with a kind of tragic irony, to prefigure one of the major political narratives of the young Soviet state: the punishment of individually blameless bourgeoisie for acts of oppression committed by their class against the working poor. A well-to-do government official gets a visit from a beautiful and enigmatic girl, whom he realizes (too late) is a kind of ghost. Badly treated by the apartment's previous tenant, she committed suicide there; now she haunts the place, leaching life-force from men like the narrator. Although the latter is not personally guilty of the girl's demise, he still suffers the consequences of the abuse she endured: a doctor advises him that the only cure for his agitated nerves is to leave Russia. Similarly, in "He," a wealthy young Lithuanian noblewoman develops a sexual obsession with a mysterious man she encounters in an old graveyard; while it is not clear whether he preys on her blood or her energy, the girl becomes prematurely aged and exhausted. Once again, the only suggested cure is to send her abroad or to mental hospitals, effectively into exile; and even this extreme solution fails. In the stories of Pavel Muratov, an art historian and antiquarian who (like Amfiteatrov) spent many years in Italy, the supernatural element revolves around *objets d'art*: "The Venetian Mirror" (1922) is a psychologically complex vignette which reflects (no pun intended) Muratov's expertise in Cinquecento culture. In this tale, a Russian visitor to Venice (already nostalgic for the Russian countryside) seeks a gift for a lover who has already returned to Russia. The mirror he finds, although aesthetically perfect, possesses a strange ability to reflect, not reality, but a person's ultimate destiny. Lena Lenchek suggests that Muratov's magic mirror is a metaphor for exile: By projecting his narrator, and the reader, into "the time of the Italian Renaissance, Muratov invites us to take refuge in an elective, timeless temporality" that revolutionary destruction cannot affect.[4] Yet Muratov's second story "The Companion" (1922), in which an obsessive art collector suffers an awful fate, seems to illustrate that anyone who seeks aesthetic bliss at the expense of others risks destruction by their own deepest desires.

The two stories by Ivan Lukash included here both belong to the famous Russian tradition of the "Petersburg tale," inaugurated in 1833 by Alexander Pushkin's short story "The Queen of Spades" and continued by Gogol (several wonderful spooky stories, including "The Nose" and "The Overcoat"), Lermontov ("Shtoss"), the works of Dostoyevsky, Andrei Bely, and many others. St. Petersburg was the capital of Russia between 1713 and 1918 (when it was renamed Leningrad), and the Petersburg tale draws almost gleefully on the contrast between the city's beautiful neoclassical buildings and its underworld of indigence, slums, and despair; between its forward-looking position as a "window onto Europe" and its terrible weather and tragic history; and not least, on its ghostly White Nights. Lukash's "Hermann's Card" (1922), written in Berlin, is doubly connected to this tradition. Not only is it a typical Petersburg tale in many ways – the loving evocation of nineteenth-century urban delights such as the city's many canals and statues, and the after-hours restaurants where the literati loved to disport themselves; the meticulous construction of a sinister, almost surreal atmosphere of pervasive gloom; and the choice of a gambler for the main character – Lukash's hero literally bumps into Hermann, the anti-hero of "The Queen of Spades." Hermann, the pragmatic but ultimately obsessive gambler and accidental murderer, emerges from the shadows of a canal to share his terrible secret with Lukash's hero. After all the somewhat self-indulgent scene-setting, the ending of "Hermann's Card" is crisp and concise – paying homage to Pushkin's style in more ways than one. The post-Revolutionary Petersburg described in Lukash's later story "The Bells" (1925) is already a profoundly

---

4. Lena M. Lenchek, "The Venetian Mirror: Pavel Pavlovich Muratov's 'Obrazy Italii' (1924) and the Literature of Art," in *Znanie. Ponimanie. Umenie*, 2015, no. 1, pp. 344–358 (p. 352). DOI: 10.17805/zpu.2015.1.35

altered place; the fabric of the city has been desecrated by violent revolution. The main character, a sculptor called Petrov, scrapes out a living by overseeing the destruction of the city's beautiful imperial statues by an organization known as "GarbIncin." (In reality, iconoclasm under the Soviet government was very restrained; very few of the main cities' tsarist monuments were destroyed or even dismantled.) Where "Hermann's Card" is a nostalgic window on the Pushkinian past, "The Bells" is an émigré's bitter vision of a spoiled homeland, recalling the nightmarish fantasies of Zinaida Gippius or Nabokov. (Zamyatin's "The Watch" also riffs on the Petersburg tale tradition, but light-heartedly, as we shall see.)

Gaito Gazdanov wrote dozens of short stories during his decades of Parisian exile: "An Adventurer" (1930) stands out among them for its speculative, almost fantastic content. The action transpires in nineteenth-century Petersburg; a conventional, but unsatisfied, society beauty on her way home from a ball observes a young foreigner sitting on the street on a freezing winter's night. Moved by concern for the stranger, but also by his mysterious charisma, Anna Sergeyevna takes him home with her only to discover that her guest is an eccentric young American called Edgar Allen Poe. Gazdanov was fascinated by and greatly admired Poe: doppelganger characters (mysterious doubles) recur in both men's fictions. A more traditionally structured ghost story, "Kum" (1929), by Georgy Peskov, pseudonym of the unjustly obscure Yelena Deisha, is a well-crafted tale of supernatural retribution. After leaving Russia in 1917, Deisha spent the remaining sixty years of her life in exile in Paris, where she published two collections of short stories. Most of her tales use eerie scenarios to capture the disturbing reality of émigré life: poverty, bereavement, want. "Kum" is one of relatively few stories Deisha set in pre-Revolutionary Russia: the word is the term traditionally used by a child's godparents to address each other. By analogy, it can also be used affectionately between close friends. In this tale, however, the friendly traditional relationship between the *kum* and his companion is distorted by a terrifying suggestion of murder, theft, and haunting.

In the remaining stories, the mystery lies in the characters' psychological motivation; excessive or misguided passion, sometimes criminal, is often the guiding factor. "The Eightieth Man" (1918), like Lukash's "The Bells," offers an unremittingly bleak view of Soviet society. Where Lukash described the hardship of ordinary urban dwellers, Krasnov's short, chilling story depicts the tribalized brutality of Soviet soldiers, sailors, and activists. Even the hero, a former White Army officer who masquerades as a soldier in order to avenge his own family by murdering Red Army conscripts, is essentially a serial killer. The Red soldiers are portrayed as primitive, conscienceless sadists; although their final act appears superficially merciful, it is intended as psychological punishment. The reader is left wondering whether Krasnov's narrator will choose exile, like his author, or suicide, or the continuation of his grisly spree. Anna, the heroine of Odoyevtseva's "By The Sea" (1928) is a Russian woman on holiday on the French Riviera with her son and English husband. She thinks she has forgotten her homeland until an encounter with a young Russian couple at her *pension*, Misha and Nina, destroys her illusions. Tantalized by Misha's obvious attraction to her, revelling in the rediscovery of her femininity and her native language, Anna indulges herself with a flirtation. But Misha falls genuinely in love with her and breaks off his engagement to Nina, who, unwilling to return to her humdrum, downtrodden existence, attempts suicide. Anna is no *Anna Karenina*, the Tolstoyan heroine who haunts this short story: terrified by Misha's declarations, contemptuous of Nina's vulgarity, she flees into the shallow civility of her perfect English marriage. Teffi's "The Mother" (1929) begins with a meditation on the sanctity of a mother's love, before describing the unrequited affection of a Russian émigré mother for her repulsive ne'er-do-well son, Paul. It ends with a straightforward murder for money. Paul shoots his pregnant wife, expecting his mother to lie to protect him. In the end, she lies for him, but not quite how he had expected.

Maternal love proves to be at least as obsessive and dangerous as Krasnov's hero's quest for vengeance.

The final two stories in this collection, Yevgeny Zamyatin's "The Watch" (1934) and "The Encounter" (1935), are also the latest in chronological terms: from their perspective, almost two decades after the Bolshevik Revolution, they can satirize both Soviet and émigré literary clichés. "The Watch" parodies the would-be exploits of a Soviet bureaucrat, whose attempt at daredevil masculinity makes him the laughingstock of his office. Although the Petersburg (now Leningrad) setting of the story is bleak enough to terrify even a Gogol character, with armed muggers haunting the snowy streets, this tale's humor outshines the impression of poverty, gloom, and political instability. "The Encounter" stages an encounter between a former officer in the tsarist secret police, once tasked with reporting seditious activity and forcing suspects to confess secrets, and a former student. Both are now in exile and, to add a certain air of unreality to their meeting, both are now acting parts in a European film set in Old Russia – the police officer is actually playing a police officer. Guilt-stricken for having previously bullied and blackmailed the former student into betraying his comrades, the officer fully expects to be challenged to a duel – little realizing that his former adversary has a different kind of re-match in mind.

No collection of this length could include all the mysteries that we would wish; many fine writers and evocative tales had to be excluded. These thirteen tales represent a fair selection of Russian émigré mystique: Petersburg revenants, grief-stricken avengers, Lithuanian vampires, flying skeletons, murders and duels, and even a ghostly Edgar Allen Poe. Read and enjoy!

Suggested Further Reading

Julie Curtis, *The Englishman from Lebedian': A Life of Evgeny Zamiatin* (Academic Studies Press, 2013)

Gaito Gazdanov, *The Spectre of Alexander Wolf*, translated by Bryan Karetnyk (Pushkin, 2013)

Edyth Haber, *Teffi: A Life of Letters and of Laughter* (Bloomsbury, 2018)

Bryan Karetnyk (ed.), *Russian Émigré Short Stories from Bunin to Yanovsky* (Penguin, 2017)

Muireann Maguire (ed. and trans.), *Red Spectres: Russian Gothic Tales from the Twentieth Century* (Overlook, 2013)

Irina Odoevsteva, *Isolde*, translated by Bryan Karetnyk (Pushkin Press, 2019)

Teffi, *Memories – From Moscow to the Black Sea*, translated by Robert Chandler, Anne Marie Jackson, and Irina Steinberg (Pushkin Press, 2016)

AUTHOR BIOGRAPHIES

ALEXANDER AMFITEATROV (1862-1938), born in Moscow and trained first as a lawyer and later as an opera singer, became a prolific writer, journalist, and critic, and an unflinching detractor of the tsarist regime. Punished with a sentence of internal exile in 1902, Amfiteatrov soon left for Paris, where he edited his own journal. Although he returned to Russia following the 1917 Revolution, his incompatibility with Bolshevism led him to move to Warsaw and Riga, where he continued writing novels, essays, and short fiction.

GAITO GAZDANOV (1903-1971), one of the most significant European novelists of the 1930s and 1940s, emigrated to Paris via Constantinople and Bulgaria. He spent most of his adult life driving a night taxi in order to stay solvent and find material for his fiction. His major novels (all recently re-translated) are *The Specter of Alexander Wolf* (1948), *Night Roads* (1941), and *The Buddha's Return* (1950).

IVAN LUKASH (1892-1940), the son of the well-known artist Sozont Lukash, graduated in law from university in St. Petersburg but was drawn to literature. After fighting in the White Army under General Denikin in the South, he left Russia for Istanbul, later settling in Berlin, Riga, and finally Paris. During his Berlin years, he became Vladimir Nabokov's close friend and favorite literary collaborator; they co-authored several screenplays together. Lukash published numerous short prose works with émigré presses and journals, many based on his own Civil War experiences, others on historical fantasy. His historical novel *The Flames of Moscow* (1930), about Napoleon's 1812 invasion of Russia, was published simultaneously in Russian and English (in Natalie Duddington's translation).

PYOTR KRASNOV (1869-1947) led a colorful but ultimately tragic career. Born into a Russian military dynasty, he became a charismatic general, later Ataman (leader) of the Don Cossacks; however, he failed to retake Petrograd (St. Petersburg) from the Bolsheviks in November 1917. After repeated Civil War defeats, he was superseded as commander-in-chief of the White Army by General Denikin. In emigration, he published many novels on Russian historical themes. During the Second World War he made the unfortunate decision to support the German invasion of Russia by leading a battalion of White émigrés and prisoners of war against the Red Army; this collaboration was intended to defeat Soviet power at any price. The price, ultimately, was Krasnov's capture and his execution in Moscow in 1947. He remains a cult figure in Russian nationalist mythology.

PAVEL MURATOV (1881-1950), born in the Voronezh region of Russia, was a scholar of Russian religious art and a specialist in Italian Renaissance texts. An art historian in the tradition of John Ruskin and Walter Pater, he spent two decades working on his three-volume *Images of Italy* (1911-1924), an account of his own travels. Together with his friend, the historian W.E.D. Allen, he wrote *The Russian Campaign of 1944-45* (1946). He died at Whitechurch House, Allen's property in Ireland.

IRINA ODOYEVTSEVA (1895-1990), born in Riga, Latvia, was celebrated in pre-Revolutionary St. Petersburg as an avant-garde poet and a great beauty. After emigrating to Paris with her husband, the writer Georgy Ivanov, she became known as a talented prose writer and as a memoirist, although their reputations did not spare the couple from suffering poverty and comparative obscurity after the Second World War. Her return to Russia in 1987 was fêted as a major cultural event.

GEORGY PESKOV (1895-1977), the pseudonym of Yelena Deisha, emigrated to France following the 1917 Revolution and spent most of her life in Paris. Her short stories feature (mostly) Russian characters facing everyday situations – sometimes in Russia, sometimes in exile abroad – that unexpectedly reveal a supernatural dimension. She published frequently in major émigré journals such as *Contemporary Notes* (*Sovremennye zapiski*), where "Kum" first appeared in 1929.

NADEZHDA TEFFI (1872-1952), the pseudonym of Nadezhda Alexandrovna Lokhvitskaya, was born in St. Petersburg into a literary family. She was already well known as a belles-lettrist, playwright, and humorist by the time she emigrated to Paris in 1919. Her short stories are famed for their often mordant wit and their comical, yet psychologically acute portraits of human foibles and episodes from émigré and Soviet life.

YEVGENY ZAMYATIN (1884-1937) was born in Lebedyan, in Central Russia and trained as a naval engineer; from 1911 onwards, his experimental and satirical short fiction drew increasing attention. *We* (first published in 1924 in Gregory Zilboorg's English translation) is still considered a classic of dystopian fiction. Although he initially supported the Bolshevik cause and the Russian Revolution (and was indeed previously exiled in 1905 by the tsarist government for his radical sympathies), he left Russia in 1931 after his books were banned by the Communist Party.

Sources

Aleksandr Amfiteatrov, "Kimmerskaia bolezn'" in S. Shargodskii (ed.), *Upyr' na Furshstatskoi* (online pub., 2013, originally published in Amfiteatrov, *Grezy i teni* [Moscow: 1895]), pp. 126-43.

Aleksandr Amfiteatrov, "On" in Amfiteatrov, *Psikhopaty: Pravda i vymisel* (Moscow: D. Ginzburg, 1893), pp. 26-37.

Gaito Gazdanov, "Avantiurist" in Gazdanov, *Sobranie sochinenii v 5 tomakh*, vol. 1 (Moscow: Ellis Lak 2000, 2009), pp. 639-59.

P.N. Krasnov, "Vos'midesiatyi: rasskaz" in Krasnov, *Step': Rasskazy* (Berlin: Grad Kitezh, 1923), pp. 59-71.

Ivan Lukash, "Karta Germanna" (pp. 216-26) and "Kuranty" (pp. 227-36) in E.B. Belodubrovskii and D.K. Ravinskii (eds.), *Nochnoi prints: Sankt-Peterburgskaia fantastika Serebrianogo veka* (St. Petersburg: Renome, 2018).

P. Muratov, "Venetsianskoe zerkalo" (pp. 21-31) and "Sobesednik" (pp. 31-47) in Muratov, *Magicheskie rasskazy* (Paris: Vozrozhdenie, 1928).

I.V. Odoevsteva, "U moria", in Odoevtseva, *Zerkalo: Izbrannaia proza*, ed. by Mariia Rubins (Moscow: Russkii put', 2011), pp. 156-66.

Georgii Peskov, "Kum", in O.R. Demidova, ed., *My: Zhenskaia proza russkoi emigratsii* (St. Petersburg: Russkii Khristianskii gumanitarnyi institut, 2003), pp. 402-14.

Teffi, "Mat'", in Teffi, *Izbrannye proizvedeniia*, vol. 4: *O nezhnosti* (Moscow: Lakom, 2000), pp. 52-59.

Evgenii Zamiatin, "Chasy" (pp. 541-51) and "Vstrecha" (pp. 562-9) in Zamiatin, *My* (Moscow: Eksmo, 2009).

HE

Alexander Amfiteatrov

Wait, let me remember… I will tell you all of it, without hiding anything – only don't rush me, allow me to remember properly how it all began…

Forgive me, if my words seem strange and wild. You cannot expect much from me, as you surely know; my family has declared me mad and they are having me treated, treated… endless treatments! I saw Kozhevnikov in Moscow and Charcot in Paris; they tried medicines, hydrotherapy, injections, hypnotism… what haven't they tried on me! Finally, everyone tired of troubling about me, and I was admitted here to this dull clinic where you see me now. It's all very nice here, and comfortable enough: only why are there bars on the windows? I won't run away; I don't care where I live. I am equally miserable whether I am free or living here, and moreover, the sight of these useless bars torments me, taunts me, oppresses me…

Perhaps my family is right and I truly am mad – I won't argue. I would even prefer if they were right; the burden I bear is too great… I would be happy to admit that the life I live is not reality, but complete hallucination, constant delirium, an endless succession of foolish ideas made flesh, phantoms of a diseased imagination. But I don't feel entitled to make this admission. I still have my memory; my thoughts are clear and logical. I was evaluated by the provincial medical board; the officials asked conventional questions, and I gave sane answers, as anyone would. It was only when the provincial marshal asked me whether I could remember my name that I started to find it funny. I

thought that he badly wanted me to answer with some crazy phrase, to betray my madness somehow: and, to make fun of the old man, I said: my name is Mary Stuart, Queen of Scots. And that put an end to it.

But you are not an official, you are not questioning me, you are not pestering me; and consequently, I have no reason to mock you or make a fool of you with silly tricks. Of course I am not Mary Stuart, but simply Jadwiga S., the youngest daughter of Count Stanislav S. I would struggle to say how old I am. You see, when all this started, I was sixteen, but since then the days and nights have flown by in such a swift and disorderly whirlwind that I have completely lost count of them. Sometimes it seems to me that my madness has lasted an eternity; sometimes, that not a year has passed since it began.

My father is a well-known man in Lithuania. Our estate, which lies close to the town of K.,[1] is a wealthy one, although neglected. Every summer we spend two months there in the crumbling tower where our grandfathers and great-grandfathers were born, lived, and died. The local peasants call our tower a castle, and rightly so: it is all that remains of a splendid structure, built in the sixteenth century by our famous ancestor, a hetman of the Lithuanian crown. It stood for two hundred years: a fire and an explosion of gunpowder in the cellars destroyed it almost to its foundations at the beginning of the present century.

The hetman chose a good site for his castle: by the foot of a high, forested hill, at a sharp bend in a limpid stream. Along the banks, to right and left, you can see the ruins of an ancient hillfort that once stood there: low brick walls with embrasures preserved here and there... These are thickly overgrown with moss, and beautiful young birches and firs have sprouted from their gaps and crannies. My sister Franja and I, with our governess Miss Emilia, loved wandering among the ruins. They rise steeply uphill from the bank and finish on the hilltop with three sturdy black walls: on one of these, even now,

---

1. Possibly Kaunas, an ancient Hanseatic town and still the second largest city in Lithuania today.

you can make out through the dirt and soot the remains of a fresco – an angel with a sword. Many gravestones with Latin inscriptions lean crookedly against this wall. Some of these have crosses scored on them, on others, miters and crowns; still others even have crude reliefs of men in clerical robes. Once, a Bernardine monastery stood here, as a gift and in the patronage of my family. It was closed down in the last century. During the second uprising, the ruins sheltered a small band of rebels; therefore Russian cannons assisted time's work of wearing down the abandoned building, by finishing it off at a stroke.

As you have already heard, I had just reached the age of sixteen. I was very lovely to look at – not as I am now. Long ago, I think, my father, when he was in good humor, would lay his hands on my auburn head and declaim with comical self-importance these famous lines by our immortal poet:

There is no earthly princess fairer than a Polish maid;
As merry as a bundle of kittens,
Her complexion like milk, with a blush like a rose,
Her eyes glow like a pair of little stars.[2]

Yet just the other day I looked in the mirror: could this be me? A bony, greenish, gnawed-looking face; deep hollows under my eyes, a jutting jaw; ears grown large and pale. How repulsive I look!

He drove me to this. *He* is a strange, mysterious being, neither man, nor demon, nor beast, nor ghost… he, daily laying his heavy hand upon me; he, in whose deadly power my soul and body lie; he, whom I fear and hate by day and by night adore with all the passion of my being; he, pitilessly leading me to an early death… Alas! What do illness, madness, or death matter to me? No horror from the visible world can frighten me. All that people call misfortune seems feeble and meaningless to me when compared to the mysteries of my

---

2. This is a stanza from the great Polish poet Adam Mickiewicz's poem "The Three Brothers Budrys" (1828), which he subtitled "A Lithuanian Ballad."

life… And yet at times I admit with shame that these mysteries are as dear to me as my own self, and that I would rather part with my life than lose them! The Hindus love to fling themselves under the heavy wheels of the proud car of the divine Juggernaut; my merciless fate rolls over me like the thundering chariot of death, driven by *him*, and I have neither the strength nor the will to step aside. With a kind of sensuous joy I await the moment when the deadly wheels will pass over me. Perhaps that is how my madness will conclude…

Now why was I telling you about the old Bernardine cemetery? Yes! Because it was there that I met him for the first time, where this began… And how did it start? Wait… Here my mind's eye is dark…

Why I climbed the hill, what I was seeking there – truly, I can't recall, but it was of no importance; no doubt I went up without any particular purpose. The sun was about to set; its big, crimson disc was swimming above the western hills: under its slanting rays the ruins seemed to rouge their wrinkles, and the gray moss over them glowed like gilt. I stood between two young poplar trees, thinking how foolish I had been to run off without Franja or our governess. Miss Emilia would be cross with me, and I ought to find them again as soon as I could. Then I noticed that I was not alone on the hill: a man was sitting on a broken tombstone by the western wall of the ruined chapel.

He startled me: for dozens of versts around, I knew everyone with the right to wear the habiliment of a nobleman; yet I had never encountered this long, lanky figure, garbed in an old-fashioned, long-skirted black frock-coat. The stranger's face was shaded by his tall, narrow top hat – also old-fashioned – pushed low over his brow. He sat with his thin legs extended far in front of him, in tall riding-boots; his arms, whip-thin, hung helplessly by his sides, resting on the tombstone. There was something not quite solid, unstable even, about the stranger's pose, that affected the eye unpleasantly; but I could not tell you exactly what this was. I decided that he must be a tourist of some sort – they sometimes wandered into our region – and out of curiosity, I watched him. He had not noticed me; or at any rate, for several minutes he did not betray by a single movement any sign of life. The sun went down. When its red orb, bound for slumber, had quite dissolved on the border between earth and sky, the stranger came to life. He shuddered and stretched, like a man who has just woken up; with a deep sigh, he made as if to rise from his spot; but he could not, and once again sank onto the plinth. Then he sighed again and, gripping the stone with his hands, flung himself on his back, then bent his torso back toward his knees, swayed right, swayed left – as if doing gymnastics to loosen limbs grown stiff from sitting still too long. The stranger manipulated himself as lightly as if he were completely boneless. He swayed to and fro for a long time; and the longer it went on, the faster he moved. The tirelessness and the horrible agility of the stranger first astonished me, then began to amuse me… I wanted to see the madman closer. I took a few steps forward; now I was standing directly opposite him, perhaps a couple of yards away, but he still paid me no attention at all. When I peeped sideways at his face, the laughter, poised to spill from my lips, froze on them; the stranger's eyes were closed, and his yellow face, beardless and whiskerless but no longer young, bore the expression of a man sleeping a deep but tortured slumber, full of nightmares and visions. It was the kind of sleep from which one longs with all one's heart to wake, but cannot. The contrast between the stranger's sleeping face and his writhing body was strange and vile. Terror seized me; I screamed.

In that instant, the stranger ceased swaying, as if arrested by an invisible hand. His cheeks quivered, his eyes slowly opened and shot a sharp, attentive gaze at my face. They were almost round, bright hazel, nearly yellow in color, like owls' or kittens' eyes, and they burned with the same cunning and predatory glow. Under that gaze I felt rooted to the earth; my legs no longer obeyed me, refusing to run, although the panicky terror, which the strange creature's awakening had suddenly roused in me, loudly urged me to do so. Unconsciously, I fixed my eyes on those of the stranger, and immediately I fancied that his unpleasant stare sank deeply into my soul, that he was reading it like a book, and that he was now its rightful ruler. Meanwhile, those cursed eyes opened wider, growing ever rounder, becoming as bright as candles... there was something tempting, summoning, and imperious in them. Instinctively I felt it was dangerous for me to obey this summons, that I must exert all the force of my soul to resist its dominating influence, yet at the same time I could not find the strength; my conscious mind protested and suffered, but my will was as if bound in irons, unable to obey my mind. It felt like lethargy.

The stranger slowly extended his hands towards me and flourished them three times in the air – and I did the same, against my will. Then he began coming closer to me, and with each step he took I also drew a step closer to him, holding out my arms before me just as he did, mirroring every one of his movements. As this strange being approached, my terror dwindled, gradually becoming a new sensation for me, at once painful and pleasant – an anxiety that tormented me with both happiness and longing. We walked on until we met face to face, breast against breast. The stranger lowered his hands onto my shoulders; my head fell on his chest; I felt as if the blood in my veins had become boiling water, surging through my body in a furiously hot stream, striving either to burst free or to suffocate me. It was an ineffable tide of passion such as I had never known existed, and if I ever loved anyone more than myself, more than this world or my life, it was this stranger during these mysterious instants of sweet madness.

I woke up in my bedroom, surrounded by my concerned family. An hour before, they had found me lying senseless at the gates before our house.

Anyone who has an inexplicable phenomenon erupt into their life, unasked-for, will certainly be oppressed and wearied by it; your habits have been sharply and rudely displaced by an influx of utterly new feelings, thoughts, sensations, and moods. It is as if you were allowed to glimpse a tiny corner of a different world, and a host of uncommon impressions burst from that corner into your mind and soul, their rich and brilliant display leaving you no enthusiasm for gray, everyday reality, nor any need of it. You have dreamed a dream that killed the truth of your life; possessed by this dream, you crave it more than food or drink. You were shown a phantom future, and by striving towards it you crush in your heart all desires and passions for your present reality as well as any memory of your past. In this ill-defined, wistful striving, you will seize on things instinctively, without knowing why; but your ignorance of your final aim will not stop you, only spur you on all the more, set you on fire and ultimately, little by little, rip you away from your life, in stubborn pursuit of a dream. Your existence, with only one foot over the threshold of normality, transforms into an ecstatic fantasy, an insane mix of melancholy and pathos, frenzied joy and stupor... Everything becomes contemptible and unneeded: the only desire that remains is the taunting vision of the mystery.

So it was for me. My cheerful nature disappeared, my life grew dull. Silently, sealed up within myself, my days dragged by after that evening on the hill. I believed devoutly that a being from another world had been with me – what did I care whether I had been dreaming or awake? I'll say it again: through the hours of torturous contemplation my desires changed so often, that as often as I cursed *him*, I passed imperceptibly to sweet dreams about *him*; at one moment I wished for *him* not to exist, to have been just a bizarre phantom of a fever dream, while at the next I craved seeing *him*, as one longs to see a real, if inexplicable, being, one visible to the eye of a living human, able to love and to be loved. When evening drew in, I grew restless. I had to struggle with myself, as with a savage enemy, not to submit to the mysterious, powerful summons, carried to me from somewhere far away and luring me... I knew where: to the hill, to the western wall. But I did not go. I still had some will of my own, and awareness enough to sense in that fateful summons something inhuman, enchanted, transgressive. At such times I hid myself away in some isolated nook and, with a thumping heart, felt my whole body shake, my teeth chatter, as if I had a fever. I would say my prayers aloud and wait for the moment to pass, for the dark dreams to drain from my soul.

I did not go to meet *him* – and then *he* came for me. One night I woke as if from an electric shock, and the first thing that I saw was two familiar, burning, feline eyes. *His* face could not be seen; therefore *his* eyes appeared to be set right into the wall as they stared long at me, unblinking and unwavering. I did not even manage to feel afraid before I was overcome by the same subjection as before... Then *he* moved away from the wall, almost as if he had walked through it; *he* leant over me, and I once again fell into the sweet faint that had seized me on the hillside.

I dreamed of choruses of triumphant music, like the thunderous chords of gigantic harps, ringing out across unfathomable voids. The sounds rose and carried me upwards, like wings. Everything around me was sky-blue, and in the boundless azure a creature floated before me that was neither a bird nor an angel – a creature with huge white wings, light and nimble, like fluff upon the breeze. Golden meteors scattered around me. Higher still, aiding and answering the harps, a silver horn blew; I seemed to be swimming in a sea of colors and sounds. It was unattainable, unearthly bliss – peaceful, warm, bright, and I thought: "How good I feel, and how happy I am!" At that very moment something painfully pierced my heart; I screamed, the bright world disappeared behind a black fog, as if the sun had suddenly been extinguished, and I woke up.

Dawn was peeping in at the window. I was alone.

Since then, I have seen *him* every night, and every night *his* embraces have borne me somewhere far from the earth, and every night I have woken alone with a bitter pain in my heart. I spent my days in gloom and agitation, waiting for the nights. Faded, dull, tongue-tied, I woke my father's concerns. Doctors diagnosed me with anemia, and began dosing me with iron, arsenic, and mineral waters. Soon I became so weak that I could scarcely move from one room to another; dizziness claimed me for days at a time; I felt sure that within another month I would be laid out for the grave...

I began to regret my young life, and I wanted to save myself. Once I overcame my enemy's influence; I did not submit to *his* captivating eyes....

"Have pity," I groaned, "whoever you are, take pity and don't destroy me... Your caresses are consuming me. I delight in them, but they are deadly. You have drawn all the blood from my heart. See how pitiful and weak I am. Have mercy on me – I will die soon." And, in response, for the first time I heard *his* voice: a noise like the rustle of dry leaves, shuffled by an autumn whirlwind.

"Don't be afraid to die. You are mine, joined with me. Like me, you will not die; and you will live, as I do. At the price of your own life, you have sustained mine, which is beyond your understanding; and afterwards you, like me, will go to another living creature and you yourself will live upon their life. Like me, you will know cold, passionless days of peace and void; and the many pleasures and wild ecstasies of the night will smile upon you, as they do on me. The golden moon will be your sun, and the blue night your daylight... Love me and do not be afraid to die!"

And for the first time I felt *his* cold lips upon my lips, and in this long kiss *he* drank my soul.

More than that I cannot tell you, for the very next day my father, after speaking with me and hearing my disconnected replies to the simplest of his questions, left me with tears in his eyes... and I realized that they thought I had lost my reason. They sent me away from the tower, started entertaining me, showing me Europe... In vain! If they could not free me from *him*, then what was the point of leaving K.! Neither traveling, nor medicine, nor prayers could help me! And who indeed would have the strength to banish *him*, a mysterious, elusive being whom none but I could see? No one!... And I will die *his* victim, and an unearthly terror seizes me, when I remember *his* dark words. "You will live, as I do..." What does this mean? Who is he? Could those old folktales really be true, and could he be... Oh, no, that would be too awful! I don't want to, I don't want to... I don't have the strength to demand a straight answer from *him*; *his* eyes are so cruel, so spiteful and vengeful, if even the thought flickers in my timid mind…

Time to say farewell. The sun is setting. *He* always comes to me as soon as the last ray fades from the belltower of that tall church, and *he* grows angry if *he* does not find me alone. Go, if you pity me. Already I feel the breath of wind that marks *his* approach, and a familiar shudder has passed through my limbs. There, now, in the corner *his* hateful eyes are glittering! Go! The time has come!

Here *he* comes… *he* comes… *he* comes….

1893

THE CIMMERIAN DISEASE

Alexander Amfiteatrov

The Earth hath bubbles, as the water has,
And these are of them.
       – Shakespeare, *Macbeth*

Oh, now that he is gone
I will rise and go on;
I must hunt another's life.
       – Goethe, *The Bride of Corinth*[1]

My dear Sasha,

Naturally you must have been quite astonished to discover that I am in Corfu, and not on Plyushchikha Street! Corfu… well, it really isn't my sort of place. I am a true Muscovite: well-fed, made idle by my easy civil service position and my bachelor comforts, sedentary, a steady chap, and not one of your daydreamers. Even in my youth I wasn't very lively, and by my thirty-fifth year I had lost all sympathy

---

1. Amfiteatrov's epigraphs from Shakespeare's play *Macbeth* (just after Banquo and Macbeth meet with the three witches, who mysteriously vanish, like "bubbles") and Goethe's 1797 ballad *The Bride of Corinth*, the tale of a young man seduced and killed by his undead fiancée, are intended to introduce the theme of supernatural incursions into the ordinary world. The girl described in "The Cimmerian Disease" shares many traits with Goethe's Bride, including her rejection of food, unnaturally cold skin, and the apparent lack of a pulse.

with your kind of people, restless wanderers through the wide world, seekers-out of powerful sensations, novelties and curiosities. Instead of stormy seas, proud Alpine summits, antique ruins and marble gods, a Russian intellectual has other pleasures: a soft couch, a blazing hearth, an interesting book and a receptive imagination.

I don't mean to deny the need for powerful sensations: but there's no obligation to experience them in person, if one can imagine them without forsaking either one's spiritual equilibrium or one's sitting-room, and moreover, at one remove… perhaps, by way of Pierre Loti or Guy de Maupassant. To expose one's own skin to extraordinary things, indeed to pine for them, to seek them out, as you and your sort will do – that's a passion I will never understand.

Such passion – forgive my vulgarity! – reminds me of an old friend of mine, the proprietress of a coaching inn in Kaluga Province who felt dull when her fleas neglected to bite her. I have not altered my opinions even now, when I have so unexpectedly swapped gray Plyushchikha Street for sparkling Corfu, where the eternally blue sky, like an inverted teacup, pours into the eternally blue sea. It's beautiful, but my imagination can conjure beauty, perhaps no better, but – how can I put this? – certainly more comfortably than reality. I miss my Moscow study, my hearth, my little couch, my office, my books and my friends, everything that the North means to me, profoundly. Traveling is all very well, but home is better; and if it were in my power to do so, I would return at once. But I cannot, and now I shall never be at home again… Never, ever!

I left Moscow without bidding farewell to anyone, rashly quitting my excellent position, abandoning an apartment paid-up a year in advance, leaving my affairs unsettled… You see, this was no pleasure trip, but a flight. Yes, I was running away. Not from enemies, not from myself; as I have none of the first, and my conscience is as good as the next fellow's – nothing to boast about, but nothing to torture myself with either. I ran away because there, on Plyushchikha Street,

I accidentally glimpsed a great secret, one I never knew and never wished to know… indeed I was afraid to know it.

For even before, in those rare moments when I chanced to think of it, this secret had glimmered in visions full of foreboding, splendidly gloomy poetry; it oppressed me, forcibly upsetting the even tenor of my life. To protect my peace of mind, to keep a healthy soul in a healthy body, I did my best to completely forget it. And for a while I did forget, and never thought of it. But the secret forced itself on me, unbidden. And it was not splendid at all, but a rather petty, gray, ordinary thing… And that was very hard to bear. You know my last apartment on Plyushchikha Street, in Arefyov's house, Number 20. It was a splendid place – spacious and bright, an absolute treasure for a lonely bachelor with homely ways. I took it in August, after the dacha season; it had just been refurbished since its former tenant, the lawyer Petrov, had left in spring. I know him well: a distinguished man and an even more distinguished carouser. When I was about to rent the apartment, I tried calling on him to ask how he had liked the place, but I found sales placards plastered outside his new flat. The caretaker told me that not long ago, Petrov had drunk himself into delirium. His family had placed him in an institution for nervous disorders.

So I moved into Arefyov's apartment without any recommendations, and I had no regrets. I felt right at home. You've visited me there – you know. On the evening of the 18th of November, I was meant to be at some friends'… perhaps even your place. But the thermometer stood at zero, which in Moscow at that time of year is worse than any frost; it means wind, and damp, and slush; clouds of fog hugged the ground, melting snow smeared the windowpanes. I stayed at home with my samovar and my book; just the day before, Denisov had lent me his copy of Huysmans' *Là-Bas* with the request that I return it as soon as possible.[2]

---

2. *Là-Bas*, an 1891 novel by French author Joris-Karl Huysmans, tells a lurid story of Satanism in *fin-de-siècle* France, featuring the historical murderer Gilles de Rais and a Black Mass celebrated in Paris.

Around ten o'clock, there was a ring at the door. Sergei announced:

"There's a young person down below… asking for you."

I was surprised.

"A lady? At this time of night?"

"Well, sir, not what you'd call a lady, as such; more like one of those *mamselles*."

"Has she been here before?"

"Not that I've noticed…"

"Ask her in."

The "*mamselle*" came in. She was a brunette; small, very slender, but quite young and very beautiful. Her eyelashes were long, dark, and so thick that they quite hid her eyes. I asked her, "How may I be of service?"

Without raising her eyes, she answered me in a very quiet and slightly husky voice:

"Petrov sent me."

"Petrov? Which Petrov?"

"The solicitor…"

"The one who used to live in this apartment?"

"Yes."

"But, if you please, I've heard that he is very ill and having treatment in an institution for nervous disorders."

"Yes."

"Well then, how on earth could he send you to me, and why would he do so?"

"He said to me: Anna! Why do you cling to me, never letting go? I have nothing left now, I've gone out of my mind; soon I'll die. You no longer have the right to torment me. Go to others! I asked him, Vasya, where should I go? I know no one except you. He answered: Go to the apartment where we used to live together; there you'll find Alexei Leonidovich Debryansky, he'll take you on."

This sounded like a lie; how could Petrov have known that I had taken his former apartment? And the girl spoke exactly like a rather forgetful child repeating its lessons; evenly, stressing each word separately, exactly like a leaky tap: drip…drip…drip…

"What can I do for you?" I asked again, but, glancing at her delicate figure, I added unwillingly, "Please sit down, and wouldn't you like a cup of tea? I'm sure you need warming up. I would even recommend you take a drop of wine or cognac with it."

She looked dreadfully chilled; her face was greenish, her lips blue, her dress soiled with mud and wet to the knees. It was obvious she had come a long way on foot.

She sat down silently. I passed her a cup of a tea. She drank it in a single gulp, as if not noticing what she was drinking. The tea and cognac warmed her; her lips grew scarlet, her amber cheeks acquired a faint bloom. She really was very pretty. I wanted to see her eyes, but her eyelashes only trembled without rising. Her gaze fell full on me just twice, sharp and glittering, but each time surreptitiously, from the side, when I was turning away. As she nibbled some bread, she did, however, reveal excellent teeth – small, even, and white.

After my guest's strange revelations to me regarding Petrov, I genuinely did begin to see her as a *"mamselle"* – one whose lover had cooled off and sent her packing. But I didn't blame Petrov for the introduction, although I continued to wonder why he had dispatched this silent female in my direction.

So instead of asking her a third time what she wanted, I became rather jolly; I decided that, as fate had sent me a romantic adventure, I should make the most of it. I am not one of your sentimental suitors; when I like a woman, I try to be witty. However, my guest never once smiled; it was as if she didn't hear my jests and compliments. Her face was fixed in an expression of dull tranquility. She sat with her hands on her knees, turned half away from me.

"I used to live here," she suddenly interrupted me, turning neither her eyes nor her head my way, as if I were not even in the room. This stubborn inattentiveness both confused and annoyed me. I thought: She's either a psychopath, or a hopeless idiot.[3]

"It's all different," she went on, gazing into a corner of the room, "different – the wallpaper, and the floors…" Aha, I thought, a vein of sentimentality – let's make use of it.

"So you are very fond of this apartment, I see?" I asked, hoping to provoke some candid outpouring from her. Without replying, she rose and walked towards the corner she had been studying.

"This is where the stains were," she said.

"What stains?" I was confused.

"Blood."

Having delivered this word abruptly, she returned to the table. I hadn't the foggiest notion what she meant. But this little fool was so beautiful, her step so light, that she stirred and attracted me until I lost my senses… and somehow, as she passed me, I embraced her and drew her head against my shoulder. I can't tell how exactly I knew my guest would not take offence at my liberty, but I was sure that she would not – and indeed, she was neither offended nor even surprised. She had cold, soft little hands and cold lips – a great charm in a woman, if she allows you to warm them.

"Now look at me," I whispered, "why are you so indifferent to me? You must have wonderful eyes. Look at me."

She shook her head stubbornly.

"Don't you want to?"

"I cannot."

"You can't? Why not?"

"It's impossible."

"Are you always like this?"

Instead of replying, she slowly raised her arms and curled them around my neck. There was no more time for questions.

---

3. Debryansky's term, "psychopath," had been known in Russian since at least 1885. Amfiteatrov must have appreciated the word, as he called an 1893 collection of short stories (not including this one, but which did contain its companion piece, "He") *Psychopaths*.

A whirlwind of passion followed. I sank to her feet, my senses ablaze, half-crazy; and she stood there, her hands on my hair, cold and unmoved, just as before. My face was burning from her kisses, but mine had not even warmed her cheeks – as if I had kissed marble.

"I must go," she said.

"Wait, wait a little…" She freed her hand.

"I must go."

"Is someone waiting for you? Who? Your husband? Your lover?"

She was silent. Then she repeated: "I must go."

"Then when will we see one another again?"

"In a month's time, I will come…"

"In a month's time? So long?"

"It's impossible to come sooner."

"Why?"

She was silent.

"You really don't want to see me sooner?"

"I want to."

"Then why put off our meeting?"

"It's not my decision."

"Is it difficult for you to come here? Will someone try to stop you?"

"Yes."

"Do you perhaps have a family?"

She was silent.

"Where do you live?"

She said nothing.

"Don't you want to say? Perhaps you're not from Moscow?"

She said nothing, tugging towards the door.

"Let me go…"

I lost my temper. I stood, blocking the door, and said: "Here's my final word: I won't let you go until you tell me who you are, where your home is, and why you can't do what you like."

Her lips trembled, and I heard her say – and I still hear her, speaking in that same level voice:

"Because I am dead."

Plainly put...

And... and I believed her immediately, and all her ways suddenly became clear to me. I wasn't afraid, except that my heart sank, as if it had tumbled into my belly, but I was astonished. I stood in silence, staring at her. She calmly walked around me into the vestibule. I seized a candle and followed her. There stood Sergei, with a strange expression on his face. He let our guest out onto the front steps. On the threshold she turned, and I finally saw her eyes... dead, unmoving eyes, which did not reflect the flame of my candle. I returned to my study, and stood there thinking:

"What has just happened? Can such things really be? Was that really possible?"

And still I felt no fear at all; but a cold, cold shiver ran along my spine, spreading up the nape of my neck and standing my hair on end. And my candle was still in my hands, and I was waving it, waving it, waving it... I was quite unable to stop... Oh, Lord! I noticed the bottle of cognac, and took a gulp straight from the neck. My teeth chattered, striking the glass.

"Master, ahem, master!" Sergei drew my attention.

I glanced at him and I could see that *he knew too*. He was as white as chalk, and his voice was cracking. And only then, looking at him, did I realize how terrified I was myself.

"Master, may I make so bold as to ask: who was that young lady who just visited us?"

I tried to control myself.

"What of her?"

"There was something very strange about her. Almost as if..."

And he hesitated, shy of using the necessary word.

"Well?"

"Almost as if she wasn't alive?"

How I guffawed – as hard as I could – for three whole minutes! Even Sergei drew back from me. Finally, he said:

"Master, you shouldn't make fun. Such things do exist. They walk among us."

"What things? Who walks among us?"

"They… the undead, I mean… And if I may say so, it's so wet outside that a good master wouldn't send his dog outdoors; and she comes along in just a little dress, with no hat… What sort of person would do that, sir?"

This struck me forcibly: who, indeed! How could I have failed to notice?

"And I'll tell you something more, sir: when just now you brought her out to the vestibule, I was standing just opposite the mirror; I could see you in the mirror, sir, and I could see myself, but not her…"

I started guffawing again; I could not control myself, and I felt on the verge of hysterics. Sergei simply stood there, with frowning brows, studying me intently: I am quite convinced that my jollity did not fool him in the slightest. That knowledge finally halted me. I fell silent, and a dreadful melancholy seized me…

"Go to bed now, Sergei."

He left. I noticed him cross himself as he went.

I don't know whether he slept that night. I certainly didn't. I lit candles on all the tables, in every corner, so that not a single dark space remained in the apartment, and until the sun rose, I paced back and forth between their glow. So that's how it is! That's it! *There* everything is just like in life, quite as ordinary; and yet it's dead, and extraordinary. I am no coward. I don't like thinking about… no, I don't like drawing any conclusions about the mysteries beyond the grave, but who doesn't enjoy a few guesses and theories? I was interested in spiritualism, theosophists, and the new magic. I follow French literature, and I am an enthusiast for its wildest occult nonsense.

There was *Là-Bas* lying on the table just there. But occultism is beautiful, vast, magnificent. There you have Saul, questioning the Witch of Endor; there you have gods, issuing forth from the earth. Manfred puts a spell on Astarte; Hamlet hears his dead father's secrets; Faust descends to "the realm of the mothers." All dramatic poses, splendid decor, meaningful words, robes and shrouds. But we know I'm no Saul, no Manfred, no Faust, just the humble and well-off director of a trading office. Supposing that even devils have their own Table of Ranks, and I've received a phantom suitable for my rank: one of the lower-class, shoddier ones.[4] But in what way am I any worse than, for example, Aratov from "Klara Milich"? And how much poetry was dedicated to him![5] "Roses… roses… roses…" a whirlwind of words, enough to take the soul by storm and bring tears to the eye. But what of a ghost that simply invites itself along and asks for a cup of tea… and leaves behind, there, a half-eaten piece of bread, still with tooth-marks…

It was all too ordinary! Even comical… Now, if only this comical ghost doesn't send me out of my mind!

The candles were guttering biliously; it was daytime. Sergei came in; he saw I had not been to bed, but he said not a word. And I remained silent.

After drinking my tea, I set off for the institution where Petrov was confined. This was not far away, on Maidens' Field, no more than five or six minutes' walk. The director of the clinic was a placid, red-haired Finn with a pale face and a beard so narrow, hanging so low, that at first glance I couldn't help thinking, "What a horse he is!"

My name surprised him greatly.

"You can't imagine how timely your visit is! Petrov has long been repeating your name to us and waiting for you to come."

"May I therefore assume that you will allow me to see him in privacy?" I asked, unpleasantly startled by this information.

---

4. The Table of Ranks, established by Tsar Peter the Great of Russia in 1722, was a 14-point scale of military, civil, or ceremonial rank, which was intended to promote talented and meritorious individuals, regardless of birth. After Peter's death the system was modified to make Russian society even more stiflingly hierarchical.

5. Debryansky is thinking of Aratov, a character in Ivan Turgenev's influential 1883 story "Klara Milich," which was filmed by the director Evgeny Bauer as *After Death* in 1915. Aratov, a reserved and bookish young man, rejects the advances of an unusual, passionate young girl; she commits suicide soon afterwards. Her specter visits Aratov in dreams, and seduces him into following her into the afterlife.

"For as long as you wish. He is a melancholic type; a calm fellow. But it is unlikely that you will be able to converse with him."

"Is he so ill?"

"There's no hope for him. He is suffering from progressive paralysis. At the moment he is in the grip of 'persecution mania,' and he turns any topic of conversation to his fixed ideas. It is madness, yet, as Polonius might say, there is method in't."

Petrov's room was tall, narrow, and long; the walls were painted blue above brown wainscoting. The entire room felt like no more than a frame for the huge, almost floor-to-ceiling window, at the foot of which stood a low-slung sleigh-like easy chair holding an unmoving bundle of brown rags. This bundle was Petrov. I stepped closer to him, overcoming the cowardly sinking of my heart. He slowly turned his yellow face towards me, a face that might have been modelled out of lumps and swellings; under the eyes, on the cheekbones, on the temples and the curve of the jaw, everywhere was swollen and flabby, all the more unpleasant to look at because, where there were no swellings, his face looked gaunt, the skin clinging to the bones.

The look Petrov gave me was both mindless, and sharp. He muttered, "Aha, you've come... I knew you would... I was expecting you... Sit down."

He and I had never been on familiar terms, but it did not now seem strange to me that he should address me so familiarly. It was as if something had happened between us that made any other form of address impossible; formalities would have sounded vulgar and foolish. We had suddenly grown close, closer than one might have thought possible, although it was not the closeness of friends. I hesitated, struggling to begin the conversation.

I could scarcely begin by saying, "So you, Vasily Yakovlevich, have been sending dead women to visit me?"

A question like that might not have seemed crazy to a madman like him; but wasn't I the one in my right mind, with a sound memory; what moral right had I to ask him questions like that? But while I hesitated, he himself asked:

"Well? Has she come to you?"

He sounded completely indifferent. But my chest tightened, and my lips went cold.

"I can see," he muttered, "I see she has. Well then? You must make peace with this, my friend, there's nothing to be done about it. Accept it."

"Of whom are you speaking, Vasily Yakovlevich? I can't follow you at all…"

"What do you mean 'of whom,' my friend? I mean her… I mean Anna."

I sat up sharply in my chair and seized Petrov by the hands. I was trembling all over. I whispered:

"So it was all real?"

And he whispered back:

"And did you think it wasn't?"

"And so, there really is a dead woman called Anna, whom you and I both know and can see?"

"There is, my friend."

"Who is she? Tell me, you madman!"

"I know who she was, but as for who she is now, that's more than you or I can know."

"Is she a hallucination? A vision? A dream?"

"No, my friend, she's no dream…" But then he thought a little and shook his head. "And yet, the devil knows; perhaps she is a dream. Only because of this dream I took to drink, and now I'm ready to die. And yet how can all this be?" He snickered: "Here I am locked in a madhouse, you have your freedom and your sanity, yet we share the same dream."

"Did you send her to me?" I reproached him heatedly. He screwed up his eyes in a way that was both cunning and foolish.

"I sent her."

"Why?"

"Because she had eaten me up, and she was still hungry – let her feed on other men."

"Feed?!"

"That's the way of it: she feeds on life. She dulls your senses, dries up your heart, darkens your brain, and draws the blood from your veins. When I die, have them do a post-mortem. You'll see, instead of blood inside me, there'll be just water and little white cells...or whatever they're called. Even under the microscope they won't find blood! Ha, ha! And the same will happen to you, my friend Alexei Leonidovich, yes, to you! She's a young woman, my friend: she wants to live, to love. She needs the life of many men, many, many..."

And he laughed so hard that all the bumps and pustules juddered on his disfigured face.

"You're making fun of me. What do you mean, she wants to live, to love? She's dead..."

"Dead, but walking around. What of it that she fired a bullet into her own temple, and was buried in a hole, or that she rotted in the hole – do you really think she's gone? You would be wrong: she exists! She shattered into billions of particles and, as soon as she shattered, she came back to life. The dead are living, my friend, all of them. Here we are talking, and between us, in this ray of light, a whole extinct tribe might be hovering. You could shape a hundred like Anna out of any handful of air..."

He made a fist and, slowly opening it, shook out his fingers. I watched his gesture with a shudder. His mad babble was beginning to oppress me.

"You think the air is empty?" he muttered. "No, my friend, it's pliable, it's alive; it teems with matter – do you understand? With obedient matter, which a mighty creative force can shape into whatever forms it wishes..."

"Good Lord! Vasily Yakovlevich!" I implored him. "Don't drive me out of my mind; I can't understand these things..." But he continued muttering:

"Diphtherias, choleras, typhus... It's all *their* work, the dead, entering into the living and bringing them over to their side. They claim others' lives in payment for their own. Ha, ha! You believe in bacilli, I'm sure, but you don't believe that the dead live, and seek revenge. See how I throw this pencil on the floor; it falls down. Why?"

"Because of the force of gravity?"

"And can you see that force?"

"Of course I can't see it."

"That goes to show that the most powerful force on earth is invisible. And if it should ever turn against you, you couldn't deflect it! Don't struggle; perish calmly."

"But I *saw* Anna," I objected, plaintively. "I embraced her, I kissed her…"

Petrov frowned. "I know it all… I've been through it… She sets your brain on fire. Others suffer diphtheria, typhus, cholera; as for you and me," he poked me with his finger, "our fate is madness."

"But why? What for?" I shouted, passionately. He frowned more deeply.

"I know why she chose me. She seeks the price of her own blood from me, my friend. Those stains there, in the apartment, have they been painted over or not?"

"I don't know… she did ask about some stains or other."

"Well, well… That was when I told her that I planned to marry, and she could do as she liked; either go back to her family, or I'd find a nice husband for her. And then when I came home from court, there she lay, with half her skull missing… And she used my revolver… And the windowsill, and the floor, red with blood and brains…"

We fell silent.

"Very well. She loved you, you jilted her, she wants revenge on you – all this I can understand. Where do I come into this, a mere bystander?"

"Because I sent her to you, my friend. I begged her for a long time to stop torturing me. What good am I to you, I asked her? You drained me dry long since. I am an empty eggshell, a husk without a nut. At least let me die in peace; leave me, I said! She told me, 'I'll go, if you give me another in your place. I am young, I haven't lived my life or had my fill of love.' So I sent her to you."

"And why me, and not to Peter, or Sidor, or Anton? Why did you think of me? How did you know I was living in your apartment? After all, you and I are practically strangers, we saw each other once or twice, perhaps three times in a year… Why me?"

Petrov shook his head vacantly and muttered:

"My friend, I myself don't know why…"

He raised his eyes to mine and began giggling.

"Alexei Leonidovich Debryansky, Plyushchikha Street, Aferyov's house, apartment No. 20! Apartment No. 20, Aferyov's house, Plyushchikha, Alexei Leonidovich Debryansky! Debryansky! Debryansky!" he repeated, louder and faster.

"What's that supposed to mean?"

He replied with a mysterious look.

"Two weeks, my friend, it's been tapping… like a telegraph…"

"Who's been tapping ?"

"Over there…"

Petrov nodded at the tiled stove in the corner near the door. "The clever chaps here, the doctor and his lot, they say the crickets were singing. But why would the crickets sing to me about Debryansky, and not about Peter, or Sidor, or Anton, as you said yourself? Who taught them what to sing? Very well! Let it be the crickets, I'll agree about the crickets – but who was it taught them, who taught them what to sing?"

Petrov looked sidelong, suspiciously, at the doors and bent over my ear:

"And I know: the force, my friend, the force taught them… that invisible force, which is stronger and more terrible than anything. Now you were frightened of Anna. What's Anna? Anna is nothing: a shape, a mold, a bubble of the earth! Anna herself is a slave. But the power, the force that gives life to these material shapes, and sends them to destroy us – 'that is the question'! It's dreadful and inconceivable! And they – as mere bubbles of the earth – cannot explain it to us. We will only find out when it's our turn to die. And I will die soon, my friend, soon, soon… And I too will be fashioned into a bubble of the earth, I too!"[6]

He opened his eyes wide, scooping the air with his hands and rolling it, like clay, between his palms. He was no longer aware of me, completely absorbed in contemplating that invisible world flurrying around him.

"Pliable, living air," I recalled, with a shudder of revulsion; I caught myself in the act of copying Petrov's motion and shaping imaginary clay between my own hands. And, in blind horror at this infectious madness, I ran from the sick man.

Sergei made inquiries about the history of our apartment. There really had been a tragic incident when Petrov was living there; the landlord had concealed it from me when I was arranging the lease so as not to scare off a tenant. Petrov's housekeeper, or, as many thought, his lover, had inadvertently shot herself. Her name was given in the registration book as Anna Porfiryevna Perfilyova, a shopkeeper's daughter from Peremysl, twenty-four years old.

And that is how I was, in one blow, knocked off the track of my peaceful life; ever since, I have lived in a place far from facts, with ghosts ruling in their place. I hadn't yet seen any ghosts, but I had already sensed them. They came between my eye and the light, like a layer of tulle; the brightest Moscow day seemed gray to me. In the clearest air, I would imagine a dim, throbbing gloom, thin as ether, and just as insubstantial… damp and slimy. I felt its touch crawling over my face. I sensed that this grayish gloom was the very mysterious substance, formed from used-up lives, ready to spawn "bubbles of the earth" of any shape, in any image, obediently serving that force which one can only understand – according to Petrov – by dying first. And I knew that within exactly one month, hour for hour, date for

---

6. Petrov cites two different Shakespearian plays in this passage: Hamlet's famous statement, "To be or not to be, that is the question", from *Hamlet*, Act 3, Scene 1; and Banquo's comment after the Three Witches mysteriously vanish, "The earth hath bubbles, as the water has" (*Macbeth*, Act 1, Scene 3).

date, as promised, that gray fog would once again send Anna from its depths to my door: an unthinking, unfeeling phantom lover, a vampire, an executioner, gifted with the inexplicably cruel and unfair power to kill me with her caresses… and why? Why?

I called on a psychiatrist; an old, gray-bearded professor with bushy gray brows over his blue eyes, whose bald skull bulged sharply forwards. After hearing me out, he thought for a long time.

"A fog," he said at last. And, in response to my questioning glance, he added, "That's all it is – see there."

He pointed to the window, gray with the milky-white gloom of cold vapors poured over it; the tiny reddish flames of the streetlights glimmered through it, as if through frosted panes.

"Englishmen shoot themselves in fogs like this, while Russians lose their minds. You are a Russian, so it follows that… I will not debate with you the reality of your impressions. In the first place, however much suffering they cause you, at the same time – isn't it true? – you want very much for them to be real, and not imaginary. Secondly, you came to see me not for a debate, but for a cure. And I will cure you. Flee from here. Flee somewhere where there's none of this…" He indicated the window again, "… and, if you can, stay there forever. Flee somewhere where there's a bright sky, a shining sun, gentle seas, palm trees and gazelles. There you will forget your ghosts. For the North – the homeland of nervous illnesses – is no good for you anymore. Your Petrov spoke the truth. Our air is alive and palpable; it abounds in spleen, cases of neurasthenia, oppressive and irritating humors. After all, we are Cimmerians. Have you read Homer?"

"A long time ago."

The doctor shut his eyes and recited from memory: "'The pale country of the dead, sunless, wrapped in gloomy fogs, where, like bats, swarms of pitiful ghosts prowl with piercing cries, filling and warming their veins with the scarlet blood they suck upon the graves of their victims.'"[7]

And, when his recitation had forced a shudder from me, the doctor chuckled and slapped me on the shoulder.

"You have the Cimmerian disease... Flee south! This illness, caused by fog and darkness, can only be cured by sun." And so... here I am...

1896

---

7. The doctor is referring to Book 11 of Homer's *Odyssey*, where Odysseus passes through the gloomy country of the Cimmerians before entering the gates of Hades, the land of the dead. The historical Cimmerians were a nomadic people who occupied part of the territory of modern-day Russia.

THE EIGHTIETH MAN

Pyotr Krasnov

He was caught red-handed. He was still holding the bloody knife, sharp and curved, and he flung it away when the soldiers seized him in their powerful grip. A crowd pressed around him and dragged him into the wide square, lit by an electric streetlamp.

The murderer, whose neat and dexterous blow with the big, curved blade had laid open a soldier's belly, turned out to be a short, sturdy fellow: strong – three tall soldiers could barely restrain him when he struggled – muscular, and agile. His dark, sunburned and filthy face bore a smallish black moustache and a short black beard; his hair was cut short, and his slightly squinting eyes burned with an unwholesome glow. He had on a well-worn soldier's greatcoat, and a hat trimmed with artificial wool.

The noise of the struggle and the yells of the crowd had brought a troop of Red Guards and sailors running up from the station; now they surrounded the captive like a solid black wall.

The captured man knew he was about to be torn to pieces or, at best, shot; but he was completely calm. Only his breathing, after fighting with the soldiers, was uneven.

Both the seasoned, hard-boiled sailors and the Petrograd Red Guards, experienced in firing squads and executions, having seen many men put to death, registered surprise that this soldier's face did not turn pale, nor did his eyes go dim, nor did he let himself droop, although his sentence had already been pronounced by the crowd of soldiers and he knew well what it was: "Shoot him!"

After all, there could be no other outcome. He had killed a sleeping comrade in the night. Why do such a thing? Undoubtedly for robbery. The murdered man had been a valued party worker, tirelessly agitating among the soldiers for the democratization of the army and the introduction of elected commanders; a man with the dull determination of a peasant, preaching hatred for officers and the need to exterminate them all like the French Catholics did the Huguenots on St. Bartholomew's Day.[1] Such a man would certainly possess money, obtained from the Party. And this experienced agitator had been struck down in his sleep with the sharp, curved knife by this small, sturdy soldier.

The case was clear. No need for a tribunal: shoot him!

But the doomed man was much too calm (and not numbed to stupor, but calm and rational) not to draw the notice of these experienced executioners.

His small, clever, piercing eyes examined the sailors and the Red Guardsmen pressed close around him with their rifles in their hands; he seemed to wish to say something.

"Comrade," a scrawny young sailor, beardless and smooth-cheeked, with the drink-ravaged face of a street thug, addressed him, "How could you do in a fellow soldier? .... Eh? Why would you do it – to rob 'im?"

"No, not to rob him," the captive replied calmly. "I have never robbed anyone."

"Well then. So why'd you kill 'im?"

"For revenge."

---

1. Krasnov has "Yeremey's Night" here. For Russian peasants, the name Yeremey, or Jeremiah, had a double application. St. Jeremiah's Day fell on May 1, marking the start of spring ploughing. But "Yeremey" was also a common nickname for idle, no-good peasants in cautionary tales. Beginning in December 1917, with the execution of naval officers in Sevastopol by their own sailors, contemporary observers began using the phrase "Yeremey's Night" to describe mass killings of officers by their troops; a blackly humorous distortion of the infamous St. Bartholomew's Day massacre of the Huguenots in Paris on August 23, 1572. These mass shootings continued through the spring of 1918.

"You knew 'im?"

"No, I did not know him. I saw him today for the first time."

"Come off it," voices broke out from the crowd. "Don't try to talk your way out of it, that won't work on us. Get the firing squad ready. Shoot him!... Why waste time on this? He killed his comrade – shoot him and be done."

The crowd fumed restlessly. Thin arms sheathed in ragged wool waved in the gloom of the night, fingers clenched into fists, gloomy, dull eyes stared wickedly; there was no hope of mercy. Death had already fastened on him and was ready to seize him in its talons; yet he still stood there, magnificently calm. He even folded his arms across his breast.

"I do not take my revenge on him only. I do not know him, I take my revenge against all soldiers. And he was not the first," he said, when their yells momentarily died down.

This case had taken an unusual turn. His guilt looked twice as grave as before, and his execution threatened to be more than simple shooting; the maddened crowd could begin slowly beating him, bringing him to the edge of death and intensifying his suffering; and he faced it. He faced it, still with the same calm.

A sturdy sailor, in a service cap worn peak backwards and a well-made black jacket, whose wide face, pale and worn – with the look of an officer, or a bosun – watched the captive with intelligent eyes and asked him slowly:

"So this was not the first man you've killed? What number was he, then?"

"The eightieth," replied the captive, unemotionally.

The crowd gasped; piling in still more tightly, they came almost close enough to touch the soldier. Even they, accustomed to all kinds of brutality, were shocked by the number.

"This is no place for jokes," said the man in the bosun's cap, sternly. "If you mean men you killed in the war, that's of no interest to us."

"No," the captive went on in the same calm tone, a barely noticeable sneer on his subtly expressive face, "this was the eightieth

Russian soldier whom I killed at night as he slept, always with the same quick knife-stroke, opening his guts."

"He's a madman," muttered the sailor in the bosun's cap.

"We shoot madmen too. But what a madman we've found! Listen, comrades, he's just gutted his eightieth soldier. Shooting's too good for him, he's got to suffer."

The crowd, which had fallen silent, exploded in howls again. Someone toward the back, trying to squeeze closer, shouted: "Does this mean, comrade, that when last night in the northern station a young soldier was slashed open and left where he lay – you did that?"

"I did," answered the captive, boldly.

"Wait, comrades, there was talk that another young soldier was killed the night before last in Sevastyanov's tavern. Can it be true that…?"

"It was I who killed him. I tell you that this one was the eightieth."

The crowd of sailors and soldiers, bloodthirsty, well used to murder, looked with curiosity and respect at this man who had dispatched, by his own account, eighty soldiers to the next world with a single knife-blow. Even by their terms, even in their stupid and crude brains, this number of crimes committed surprised and intrigued them.

"Well, this is a pretty tale. Comrades, let him make his confession before he dies, what he meant by putting away eighty poor-bastards-of-soldiers. And then we'll discuss how to make him suffer for it."

The warm, gloomy night hung over the town. All the streets were sleeping; only this grim crowd, churning dully and breathing heavily, piled one upon another, trying to get a closer look at this remarkable man; they pressed up against each other and reveled in the sweet expectation of his cruel torture and execution.

"For starters, might you tell us who you are?" the bosun asked.

The captive did not answer immediately. He considered, letting his stern, noble head fall briefly onto his bosom. Then he raised it and said, staring proudly into the crowd:

"I could lie, give any name. My papers are another man's, some other soldier's. They belong to the first man I gutted, he whose name

I live under, but I do not want to do that. Before I die, the troops should know the truth."

He paused. Tensely devouring him with their eyes, panting right into his face, the sailors and Red Guards pressed close around him.

With an authoritative light in his eye, like one accustomed to commanding others and subordinating them to his will, the captive surveyed the crowd. Then, calmly and distinctly, loudly and with emphasis, pronouncing every word clearly, he announced:

"I am Staff Captain Konstantin Petrovich Kuskov, an officer..."

An explosion of fury stopped him from finishing. Once again, hands waved in the air, some clenched their fists, others brandished weapons, and again vicious yells broke out:

"An officer! Just look at him! Comrades, shooting's too good for this one!... He should be killed in a way they'll remember... if one of us kills his brother soldier, we might have mercy on him, either because his reason was darkened, or out of allowance for the people's ignorance, but here's an officer! An educated man!"

"No, comrades, let him explain first why he took to oppressing us like this ... with these murders."

The voices fell quiet again. Their thirst to hear something so horrible and extraordinary forced them to fall silent and listen to this calm man.

"Tell us what it was that made you slaughter so many soldiers?" asked the bosun.

"Certainly... Three months ago our regiment left its position without authorization and was withdrawn to the town of Ensk, my native town, where my family lived: my elderly mother, my young wife and our three children. I hadn't seen my family since the war began three and a half years before. It was terribly shameful to return home without a victory, without permission, like deserters. We officers had tried to talk the soldiers round, persuade them not to do it, but the regiment was already led by a self-appointed committee and we couldn't achieve anything. They didn't listen to their officers – they insulted them..."

"We know their lot always blame the soldiers. To listen to them, it was all the soldiers' fault we lost the war," voices came from the crowd.

"Wait, comrades, let's hear him out."

"And you, comrade, be quicker about it."

"Very well. I won't detain you. In Ensk, disturbances broke out. They killed the regimental commander and almost all the officers. They broke into my apartment, looking for a machine-gun. Before my eyes they killed my mother. Then they seized me and held me by the arms; they violated my wife until she died in the villains' clutches. They did the same to my twelve-year-old daughter, and they killed my eight-year-old son and my four-year-old daughter, cut them to pieces. Afterwards they set me free. They said: 'Look on and learn from the soldiers' lesson…' Oh, I learned well. Our regiment had disbanded and I could not find the villains. So I swore to revenge myself on all those men who confuse their fellow soldiers' souls. I put on a soldier's greatcoat, bought that sharp dagger, and set off to wander among the market stalls, where enlisted men were selling off military uniforms; the train stations, where deserters gathered; thieves' dens. I crowded in with soldiers at political meetings; I listened to agitators wherever I went. And when I heard someone calling for rebellion, for fraternization with the enemy at the front, for the murder of officers, I never let that man out of my sight. And that night, or the next one, in the station amid a multitude of sleeping men, in a hostel, at a halting-stage or in some den, I would steal up to him where he slept and wreak my bloody vengeance with that same skilled stroke of my knife. I learned to act so quickly and dexterously that sometimes I carried out the deed in the big, badly lit waiting room of a railway station when people were still walking around. I only waited until the nearest ones were asleep. I resolved to kill eighty men, because there were eighty men who caused the trouble in our regiment, spreading murder and violence. I had no fear of being captured, because what is death to me? Nothing. What suffering can touch me when I remember the agonies of my wife and daughter, my own agony? I crave bodily pain. Torture will gift me bliss and redemption... I wished only to fulfil my quota. To kill eighty men. Thus until today I was restrained and cautious. The man I killed today was the eightieth and I could allow myself a small luxury: to approach and kill a sleeping man before the eyes of his wide-awake comrades... And I could have walked off... They were afraid of me. But I threw my knife away. And now I welcome death. I welcome torments... I crave death... I dream of the saving agony of torture..."

Heavy silence and ragged breathing, from many mouths and noses, greeted his tale. And in this silence lay a dull, sluggish thought. It was the envy of the professional executioner for the amateur who outshines him. The dark thought suggested that for this man, life was more painful than death and thus, if he must be punished, the punishment of staying alive would be a far greater torment than execution...

Respect for this man, who scorned death and murder, crept across many of the faces. Artists gazed upon an artist.

Wet gloom hung over the dirty square. Streetlamps flickered feebly, leading away into the black distance, towards other squares and main streets of the now sleeping town, full of massive edifices, palaces, churches, full of sleeping people.

Staff Captain Kuskov lowered his head and waited to be seized, beaten, tortured. Only the first blow would be hard and painful, he thought; then the stupor of semi-consciousness would come, and pain would lose its power.

And he waited for that first blow.

But it did not come.

He raised his head. The place before him was empty. The crowd of sailors and Red Guards had left the square, silently, hanging their heads.

He understood. The people's court had sentenced him, without a word, to its cruelest torture: life.

Kuskov once again sank his head onto his bosom and quietly left the square. He entered a narrow, cramped street. His shadow, cast by the streetlight, loomed sinister on the muddy ground, stretching to the walls of houses, hesitating there, and vanishing. But the Staff Captain himself could not be seen.

The shades of night had swallowed him.

Konstantinovskoye Cossack stanitsa
March 1918

HERMANN'S CARD

Ivan Lukash

In the year 1881, the People's Will Executive Committee wanted to make all of Russia rise in rebellion, but does anyone really know what this Executive Committee was?

Its agents were scattered through the whole Empire, even hanging their proclamations on St. Petersburg's Nevsky Prospect; pale, long-haired people began visiting the workers on the factory floors; a great bomb blast shook the Winter Palace, also killing innocent young soldiers of the Finland Regiment's Life Guards.

It was a terrible time. No one knew who was on the Executive Committee, but it was well known that the Committee wanted to make all of Russia rear up on its hindlegs; a manifesto had already been released calling on peasants to take their axes to hack at and slash the gentry throughout every province, to kindle fires everywhere, and hang the clerks and judges, and on soldiers to bayonet all their generals and kill the Tsar himself, so that all would be as it was under Yemilyan Pugachyov: liberty, and rebellion, and joyous retribution.[1]

Now, the principal agent on this Committee was Sofia Perovskaya.

She was a soft-looking thing, well-born, from a noble family. Her little face was delicate and sad, except for the severe line traced above her brows. Her whole complexion glowed, like a white snowflake.

---

1. Yemilyan Pugachyov was a Cossack peasant who, pretending to be the Tsar Paul III, led a rebellion against Catherine II in 1773-4. He was executed in 1775.

ЦАРЕУБІЙЦА

After they killed the tsar, Sofia Perovskaya and the other regicides were brought to the Semyonovsky Regiment's parade ground for execution.[2]

She was taken there in a tall black tumbril, her back to the driver, with a gray signboard nailed to a pole above her head, listing all her crimes against the state.

They were all hanged at dawn. But Sofia Perovskaya, when she went up on the scaffold, suddenly waved a white handkerchief – as the drums rolled, and the cordons of Guards shoved the crowds back with their rifle-stocks – and thus she was hanged without uttering a word, a canvas sack over her head, under the juddering gallows-pole. All the others writhed as they dangled inside their sacks, but she huddled up on herself as she hung from the gallows, and never moved again, just like a smothered kitten… And some old folk say that the hanging didn't kill her at all. It did happen in the year 1775 that, in a ravelin of the Peter and Paul Fortress, the Queen of all the Russias, the Princess of Vladimir, known as Yelizaveta Tarakanova, was supposedly drowned in a flood, yet the old people say that she never really drowned, and that she still walks St. Petersburg…

And of Perovskaya it is said that whether or not she died that day, only her specter is ever seen…

In the month of March Petersburg is dark; the sea wind howls and lashes the roofs, wet snow falls in heavy flakes, blinding the eyes, and the snowy gusts put out the dreary streetlamps. Streets are empty; only the snowy whirlwind roams them… On nights like these, Sofia Perovskaya appears on the arched bridge over the Yekaterinsky Canal. She stands on that bridge where she once waved her handkerchief, giving the signal for a bomb to be hurled under the Tsar's black sleigh… A small, huddled shade, just like a smothered kitten, her white hair windswept, and her little face shining dreadfully with a cold and lusterless glow…

---

2. Sofia Perovskaya was executed in 1881 for the assassination of Tsar Alexander II, along with four other members of the terrorist group known as the People's Will.

And in the glass-covered arcade of the Alexandrovsky market, from where a dark little passage still leads to a bazaar, the very same arcade with a painting of two angels in blue chasubles, bearing the Icon of Our Lady of Smolensk into the clouds, a certain rag-and-bone man, eccentric, and philosopher, Sapunkov by name, showed me a bronze figure of a dancing harlequin, mounted on a green malachite stand. And Ivan Fyodorovich Sapunkov assured me that, at Shrovetide, this bronze harlequin flees from his shop every night to cavort in masquerades… And perhaps that story is true: how can one really tell, beneath a mask, who might be dancing the polka through those gloomy halls?

And at the Academy of Arts, on the Vasilyevsky Island embankment, where the two sphinxes still lie in scornful slumber on their stone plinths, their taloned paws gripping the granite, they say that on those nights when the river Neva bursts its banks, a knock may be heard on the great gates.

One night, it is said, the porter pressed his ear against the iron lock and called:

"Who's that knocking?"

And perhaps it was the roaring of the wind, or the tumult of the Neva's waters, but he seemed to hear a voice reply:

"I am knocking, I – Kozlovsky the sculptor, from the Smolensky Cemetery, all soaked and frozen in my grave… Open up!"

The porter crossed himself and fled away from the lock, because that same Kozlovsky who knocked had died fifty years before; his granite tombstone still bore this inscription:

Under this stone,
Lies one who vied with Phidias,
The Russian Buonarotti…[3]

---

3. Mikhail Kozlovsky (1753-1802) was a celebrated Russian neoclassical sculptor, educated in Paris, later a professor at St. Petersburg's Academy of Arts. His sculptures were based on classical myth and legend, including his monument to General Suvorov in St. Petersburg's Field of Mars. Phidias was a Greek sculptor active in the fifth century BC, whose statue of Zeus at Olympia was counted among the Seven Wonders of

Such things may happen, of course… And whether they do or not, it was certainly true that at three o'clock in the morning of a white night the famous card-player Sokolovsky was walking along the English Embankment.[4]

Every man has his own profession. One man builds stone houses, another scribbles verse, a third spends his whole life operating shiny metal levers in a foreign machine, a fourth hangs men by judicial decree, a fifth chooses to cut men's throats…

Sokolovsky had never had a real profession: he was a card player, and he lived by cards. Thanks to cards, he was forced to retire from his cavalry regiment at the rank of captain. Thanks to cards, he had sold two estates to timber merchants to be felled for the sawmill, one in Kharkov Province and one in Samara Province. Thanks to cards, while still a young man, he had lost his young and gentle wife, Zinaida Sergeyevna, who died of consumption after many weary and sleepless nights awaiting his return from his clubs.

Cards were his art, his beauty, his pleasure. He lived on a generous scale, but kept his distance from others. His luxurious, somewhat gloomy flat on Ofitserskaya Street was familiar to all the young officers, although they only stayed until a certain hour, when their reserved host would rise and say with chilly amity:

"And now, my dear sirs, it's time for us to be on our way, to Cuba or Donon…"[5]

The cut of his jackets was much copied, and he was the first to adopt the custom of wearing a starched shirt-front with white gaiters and a monocle on a black silk ribbon.

---

the Ancient World. Michelangelo Buonarotti (1575-1564; Lukash mistakenly writes 'Bonaparte') was a great Florentine sculptor.

4. Because of St. Petersburg's proximity to the Arctic Circle, for almost three months every summer the sun never really sets, causing a phenomenon of lingering twilight known as the "White Nights."

5. Both were well-known St. Petersburg restaurants near the Moika Canal. In the nineteenth century they were frequented by aristocrats, artists, musicians, and a host of literary types.

Is there a Petersburg native who doesn't know or remember Sokolovsky? He came to all the private views, the opening nights, the races. He always appeared looking slightly pale in one of his irreproachable black jackets. He also had a habit of thoughtfully biting the gold knob of his cane. With his leonine appearance and quiet manners, he could have been taken for a great artist.

And, indeed, he was an artist. He always played honestly. In the long, black nights, he never let himself doze, calculating with feverish enthusiasm the countless permutations of *Chemin de Fer* and Macao. He was burning himself up slowly, but the dark flame devouring him was revealed only by the heated glitter of his ever-sorrowful eyes, and by a faint, barely perceptible tremor in the corners of his coolly compressed lips.

Sokolovsky was a celebrated gambler. Many fortunes had melted in his pale, slender hands. People had shot themselves because of him. Others had begged on their knees, writhing at his feet. And his mute and sinister shade overhung the entire trial of an insurance company director who had run through the company's assets at the card table.

As a gambler, Sokolovsky was merciless. He had long since grasped the alluring secret of packs of cards, as they rustled on the green cloth of the card tables, the languid knaves and pale queens with strange white flowers in their delicate hands, and the gloomy kings, and the peculiar aces, and the flickering red and black tens, and twos, and eights...

At the card table in the wan and gloomy candlelight, when the players' voices grew hoarse and their fingers hooked like grasping claws, and their eyes wandered over the piles of gold and the packets of credit-notes, Sokolovsky, flinging down a card with a calm and elegant gesture, sometimes caught himself thinking:

"And what if I am now dealing out someone's life? Perhaps we are playing with souls, not cards... In the infinite randomness of combinations, perhaps, we card-players are creating and destroying millions of lives and millions of deaths... Perhaps the gods, like us, are players, playing blindfold with us and with the whole universe, their cards face down..."

It should be said that Sokolovsky could hold in his mind about three thousand combinations of *Chemin de Fer* and that people were afraid to sit down to Macao with him...

And then, suddenly, chance turned against him. At first it was a ruddy, whiskerless cavalry officer who beat all his cards before dawn three nights running. Then it was a fleshy comedian from the Alexandrinsky Theatre, who looked like an easygoing good sort but was in reality ill-tempered, cunning and greedy. The comedian, without yielding him a single card, swallowed audibly and puffed, testing his gold five-ruble coins with his short and stumpy fingers. Then it was a race-horse breeder, then a dissipated sales clerk, half-drunk, sweaty, and cravenly impudent.

It had become too much. Last week at his club on Nevsky Prospect, someone had shouldered him away from the table without even apologizing. He began to notice contemptuous and mocking glances. He stopped gambling. The day before, he had clearly heard a student in a dark-blue frock coat, with a flabby, eyebrowless, and womanlike face, say behind his back:

"A fallen star. That's the very man who used to be Sokolovsky..."

"I still am, I am..." said Sokolovsky to himself, knocking his cane against the flagstones of the embankment. "I will prove myself yet, I'll have my revenge..."

Resentment spurred him on. He doffed his top hat. He walked aimlessly along the embankment, sadly conscious that he would once again enter the gambling house and again stand there with pinched lips, like a lackey at the dining-table, and people would elbow him carelessly. But he would not be seated to play, he would be afraid to sit because all his money, down to the last three-ruble credit note, was squandered...

It was a white night.

On such nights, the wan glitter of dawn shines for a long time in the mirrorlike windows of the low palaces along the English

Embankment, like the embers of a smoky crimson bonfire in the pale sky.

On such nights, Petersburg silently softens in the transparent silver haze of that half-light, half-darkness, when the sad gaze of the ladies of the night through the gauze of their veils is so sorrowful and so seductive; and in the zoological gardens, the scraggy white she-bears pace, staggering softly around their cages, deceived by the noiseless twilight.

On white nights Petersburg quietly shimmers from within, like a pale icon lamp. On white nights, everything is smoke and mirrors, half-heard, half-phantom, silvery visions and sorrow. On white nights, everything quivers gently, everything floats lightly and dimly along in a pale current of houses, palaces, colonnades, avenues, and railings vanishing into obscurity. In this silvery, glimmering gloom, Petersburg slips its moorings. Petersburg stirs silently. On white nights, Petersburg dies – quietly and tenderly, without noise or palpitations, like a pale icon lamp burning all the way down.

The ireful emperor is dying, his horse rearing over the dim precipice.[6] The dark sphinxes are dying, twisting their stone lips in an eternal and mysterious sneer. And the cast-iron angels holding their huge quenched torches over St. Isaac's Cathedral are dying too…

On the white nights, St. Petersburg dies – dies sweetly and painlessly…

Sokolovsky walked along the embankment as if through the depths of mirrors; he cast no shadow in the shimmering silver gloom.

Above the pallid Neva he paused, placing a hand on the granite wall; its rough stone was covered in cold dew.

At Millionaya Street he crossed over the wet pavement towards the Lebyazhaya Canal.[7] And when he stepped under the tall and dark

---

6. This is a reference to the French sculptor Falconet's equestrian statue of Peter the Great, immortalized as the titular Bronze Horseman which comes to terrifying life in Alexander Pushkin's 1833 poem.

7. It is no coincidence that the stranger is on his way to Millionaya Street when he meets Sokolovsky. Princess Golitsyna, the real-life model for the title character of the

archway, biting the knob of his cane, he thought he saw the shadow of a man coming his way.

Sokolovsky peered vaguely into the dimness. The strange passerby approached him as if through dull mirror-glass. His black cloak drooped off one shoulder and trailed on the ground. Under the brim of his hat, his black eyes had a sinister, threatening gleam. Beneath the stranger's cloak, Sokolovsky noticed the silver tassels of splendid aiguillettes; strange, old-fashioned tassels, he thought, of a kind no longer worn. And a strange costume, as if for a masquerade.

The passerby made for him, crossing his arms over his breast:

"Wait, Sokolovsky! Are you seeking a lucky card?"

The gambler, always so calm, shuddered at the other's cold, hollow voice, but he swiftly mastered himself and asked in a superior tone, replacing his hat:

"How would you know what I might be seeking? And why do you address me so familiarly, as if we were guests at a masquerade? Who are you?"

"Odd that you didn't recognize me. I wear a mask, eternally, because I am a gambler just like you... I am Hermann."

"Hermann... Wait, Hermann? I don't recall any such surname. It has something old-fashioned about it. I have known none such... I don't remember ever meeting you at the card table."

"Nor have I met you, but I am with you always, because you are a gambler. And can you really have forgotten that I know the three lucky cards?"

"You seem to be making fun of me... But never mind, tell me which ones they are. I'm curious," requested Sokolovsky, suddenly dry-mouthed.

"The three, the seven, the ace."[8]

Countess in Alexander Pushkin's story *The Queen of Spades* (1833), had a house at 30 Millionaya, where she died at the age of 96, outliving Pushkin himself. In that story, Hermann frequently lingers outside the Countess' house.

8. These are the winning cards confided to Hermann in *The Queen of Spades* by the Countess' ghost.

"The three, the seven, the ace… Aha… Three cards… Very well, I'll remember them. I thank you; I'll test them. I have lost all my money and will win it back, I am going off to play, I thank you…"

"Don't thank me. I will come with you. I too will play."

In the pale silvery shimmer, they hurried through the empty Field of Mars, just like phantoms from a strange masquerade, or like shades, sliding through the mute depths of mirrors; the slender gentleman in the black tailcoat and top-hat and the short officer in an old-style black cloak and black cap…

In the Concordia Club on Nevsky Prospect, in the rear courtyard of a massive house on the corner of Mikhailovsky Street, all the wan electric chandeliers were shining, because all the blinds were drawn. The gambling room was submerged in a fog of tobacco smoke. Pale-faced gamblers were leaning over the long green table; the light of the chandelier glittered dully on their hair.

The game was proceeding wearily and wordlessly; a gray, prosperous-looking man in a black buttoned-up frock coat, the trustee of several orphanages, had lost three hundred thousand to a famous lawyer in a crumpled starched shirt and a wide-cut black tailcoat, whose puffy, yellowish face resembled an actor's…

Sokolovsky, placing his top-hat and cane on the shelf below the mirror in the anteroom, squinted at the glass. Seeing his pale, reserved face reflected in the lamp's wan glow, for a moment he did not recognize himself; he smoothed his hair and wondered, "Well, where's my companion?"

He looked around. His mysterious companion was standing beside the heavy door-curtain with his back turned, his black cloak draped over his arm. Sokolovsky took a step forwards, and his companion stepped before him into the smoke-filled room…

"I'll stake twenty thousand," Sokolovsky said, dropping heavily into the chair opposite the lawyer. Sokolovsky caught his breath briefly, clenched his teeth and sent a wandering glance in search of his companion's black shadow. The trustee of the orphanage passed him the pack, and Sokolovsky, glancing at his black, tightly buttoned frock-coat, whispered, "Are you here, Hermann? Look, I'm playing."

"Your three has won," said the lawyer, squinting carelessly and sleepily at Sokolovsky, pressing his puffy lips together and passing him a packet of credit notes and gold across the table.

"I'll stake forty," Sokolovsky muttered through clenched teeth, pushing his winnings away from him. A single gold coin rolled along the green broadcloth and fell on the parquet with a pure, sad ringing note. Sokolovsky shuddered.

"Your seven has won," said the lawyer with a note of surprise, half-opening his swollen eyes. His crumpled, yellowish face frowned in irritation.

Chairs scraped all around. A few men, after glancing over, rose to their feet. They crowded around Sokolovsky.

"I'll stake it all," he sighed, hoarsely, dry-mouthed.

The game continued in the charged silence of extreme tension; when a gambling hall falls quiet, the silence may be ghastlier even than the final moments of an execution, the last convulsion of a murder. Someone whispered: "What a terrifying game."

"The ace is mine!" Sokolovsky cried, rising. "I've won…"

"No, you've lost," the lawyer raised his voice mockingly. "Your card is not an ace, but a queen."

"A queen? Which queen? Oh, yes – the Queen of Spades. I forgot, I forgot. It's the Queen of Spades, the cursed murdered hag has taken my last stake – I forgot, I forgot…"

He rose from his chair, gazing around. He cast a dreadful look at the clean-shaven lawyer, as if he saw before him instead the monstrous dead old woman, rouged, with her flabby yellowish face, or death itself, winking mockingly at him.

"The masks, the masks!" Sokolovsky cried madly.

He covered his face with his hands and burst out laughing… Or perhaps it was not him, but someone else laughing in that smoke-filled room?

You may remember that the eternal Petersburg tale *The Queen of Spades* breaks off with these lines:

Conclusion

Hermann lost his mind. He is kept in Room Seventeen at the Obukhov Hospital, refuses to answer questions, and mutters with unusual rapidity, "Three, seven, ace! Three, seven, queen!"

Now the card-player Sokolovsky is also in the insane asylum.

1922

THE BELLS

Ivan Lukash

The monument to Krusenstern on the 11th Line of Vasilyevsky Island, opposite the Cadet Corps, is covered in snow.

Ice coats the bronze letters:

"To the First Russian Admiral to Circumnavigate the Globe…"

The admiral's cast-iron blunt-nosed shoes and the cast-iron foot-straps of his narrow trousers are barely visible under the snow; a white wart sprouts on the admiral's nose.

Before the stern portico of the Mining Institute, Hercules, in the act of choking Antaeus, and the abduction of Proserpine are buried in snowdrifts. On Hercules' muscular black calf, a chipped corner is turning white, just like frozen meat, and Antaeus' black head protrudes from a drift: mouth crooked, eyes bulging, suffocating in snow.

In the mornings, making his way to GarbIncin, he trudges past the yellow buildings of the Academy of Arts, past the sphinxes brought from Thebes.

Heavy letters are screwed onto the blackened marble above the Academy's vast gates, "To The Free Arts"… The sphinxes are like granite cats, powdered with snow.

He runs a fingernail over the hoar-frosted granite of their plinths. Like a chisel, his nail traces a letter in the silver fluff: N, over and over again…

Crossing the deserted court, where a plank bridges two snowdrifts, he pushes the brown oak door inwards after a long effort – it squeaks

just as excruciatingly as it did a hundred years ago – and he enters GarbIncin.

He works in GarbIncin.

GarbIncin is the place where the two-headed eagles, statues, marble plaques, monuments, bronze porphyry, broken carriage-lamps with gilded monograms, and other regalia of the overthrown Empire are stored.

All four hooves flung upwards, the steed of Emperor Nicholas I has toppled over. Through the dust, the bronze of the horse's scored and swollen flank and the pointed toe of a copper shoe emit a yellowish gleam.

The Emperor's head, wearing a Horse-Guards shako, has been wrenched off and rolled under the table, where its bulging eyes glare out of the gloom.

GarbIncin took Nicholas I from Mariinsky Square. The Emperor will go in the smelting furnace.

Imperial eagles have been propped against the wall. Some of the spikes have been broken off their wings, their talons clutching orbs and scepters have been twisted open.

The eagles of Alexander the Blessed hold their iron wings straight and strong. Sharply angled, like two humps, the wings of the black eagles from the time of Nicholas I are tucked downward, and the eagles of the last emperor are curly and insubstantial, just like the imprints on a copper kopeck.

The eagles of Elizabeth I and Catherine II, made of an ancient alloy of bronze and gold, wink through the dust with unextinguished brilliance and ardor.

Beaks agape, the iron Maltese eagles of Paul I roll up their tongues like venomous snakes.

From a dark corner, a marble Catherine II benevolently extends her majestic hands. Her fingers are chipped and blackened, the marble covered in feminine dimples, her palms charred. The sallow porphyry is cut and crisscrossed with an intricate web of obscene inscriptions.

The Empress Catherine had been banished to GarbIncin from that spot by the General Staff Building which Red Army sentries had marked out for calls of nature.

Catherine's lips are curved in a mellow smile across her right cheek – her left cheek has been hacked off, as if gnawed by a silver wolf-cub.

The bust of a cast-iron general has been flung down on its belly.

It was brought from the Vyborg Side. Cobblestones have holed its back. The bust is empty inside, the ragged cast-iron edges on its back gaping like a trap-door into a spacious cellar. Its dented head has a high, swollen forehead, like that of a dwarf or a freak. On its breast is a cast-iron ribbon with many cast-iron stars, and a cast-iron inscription is engraved on its base: His Highness Prince Kutuzov-Smolensky.[1]

Raising his feet high, he steps around the dusty eagles.

That black eagle, which once looked down on the Decembrists, was toppled off the apothecary's storefront on St. Isaac's Square; these were culled from Vasilyevsky Island; two gilded and grandiose ones were broken off the lamps on the bridges; that bronze eaglet, a fierce fledgling, was unscrewed from Liteyny Prospect.

There are eagles from armories, from pediments, from the façades of steel foundries and rolling mills, from barracks and hospitals.

GarbIncin is a graveyard office, where the Russian Empire is sold off for scrap.

"Comrade Petrov."

"Yes, sir?"

The door has opened a crack. A sinuous, swarthy limb grips the jamb... Just visible are the black sleeve of a jacket, bony fingers, fingernails catching the light. This is the man known as Comrade

---

1. Field Marshal Mikhail Kutuzov (1745-1813) is remembered as the brilliant general who defeated Napoleon's 1812 invasion of Russia. He received the title of Prince Smolensky for the battle in which Marshal Davout's baton was captured (see later in this story).

GarbIncin himself. Like a Chinaman, Comrade GarbIncin has long, sharp nails.

"Comrade Petrov, be so kind the day after tomorrow – no, tomorrow…"

Comrade GarbIncin steps into the storeroom.

His eyelids lie in wrinkled folds; hot furrows have baked two deep lines down to his dry, singed lips. His black mane is pulled back from his dark brow. Comrade GarbIncin has a narrow, caudate head.

"Be so kind tomorrow to free up a place in the storehouse. The GarbIncin Board has resolved to take down the bells from the Peter and Paul Fortress."

"The bells?"

"Yes, you can dump them over there, on the monogrammed carriage lamps. You'll have to do something about the wheels, chains, and pulleys; the bells' mechanism is cumbersome. Please note one more thing: send the four coats of arms, Nicholas I's head, the horse's leg, and the five monograms to be melted down…"

"Yes, sir, I've made a note."

Comrade GarbIncin looks at his Chinese fingernails, distractedly taps nail against nail and turns his back on Petrov.

GarbIncin's black back is hunched. The points of his shoulder-blades judder as he walks.

But perhaps, flattened under his black jacket, a pair of skeletal wings are crammed. And as soon as the first wing breaks free, everything will fall in ruin; and when the second unfurls, glaciers and darkness will gush forth…

✳

In the frosty silence of the embankment, the pealing of the bells of the Peter and Paul Fortress flowed long and clearly, like icy water splashing into an urn.

The faintest chimes trembled in the radiant dusk over the downy whiteness of the snows; the frosty silver powdered down, ever more slowly; frail and lingering, the bells poured out, chimed, with a sorrowful and hesitant refrain, the hymn "How Glorious Is Our Lord…"

The lingering vibration, the trickling silver, the lingering sorrow – chiming the measure of our days…

Saint Petersburg, the Northern Commune, the year 1921 from the birth of Christ…

On Kronverksky Prospect, the palings have collapsed. Wooden houses stand empty, with fallen-in roofs and old rags in place of windows. The glass in the houses has been smashed by coffins.

On the abandoned avenues, stove-pipes poke out of the roadbed, just as if a vast, quiet conflagration has passed lazily over the capital.

Saint Petersburg lives on the bitterness of ash, on raw charm. Wasteland is laid bare. There are piles of bricks in the grass. Railings rust.

Dead horses have been left on the pavements. The horses' flanks are swollen, their jaws are bared, and death has tensed their skeletal legs. Silent cavalry squadrons have galloped over the city in a silent charge, scattering equine carcasses across the paving stones.

The sculptor Petrov, his face translucent from hunger, wandered through the capital in a woolen overcoat.

By Tuchkov Bridge a rotten, frozen potato was stuck against the window of the Children's Paradise toy shop. Gray ooze crawled slug-like down the glass. N – the trace of a nail on rime over granite… She used to press her childish brow against the glass of Children's Paradise.

At the Filippov Bakery, the warped copper railings by the doors have turned green. Wooden tables have been set out inside the bakery, under a sign reading "Communal Kitchen."

In the cold twilight, side by side with people as gloomy and pale as he, Petrov warmed his thin hands on the hospital-issue tin pail and doubtfully spooned chunks of dark horsemeat out of briny water. The silent cavalry charge had galloped over the capital; the horsemeat was the Commune's ration…

Blind, boarded-up windows, extinguished lanterns bowed under the weight of ice.

In the wasteland of the streets, lonely canvas signs announced in brown paint: "The Consumers' Cooperative," "District Store No. 5." Behind the windows, in enormous corn-bins, lay frozen cranberries and potatoes. The cranberries, like congealed blood, are mixed with snow: frozen blood is the Commune's ration…

Shots and silence. A shining silence settles on Saint Petersburg. The capital rusts, laying bare its avenues and lines, the graceful enfilades of its palaces, beautiful, bright, and dead – like N… N – the trace of a nail on rime over granite.

Above the wasteland of the Prospect of Red Dawns, the wan sunrises and sunsets come and go. Only the dawns mark the succession of dead days, only the dawns and the chiming of the bells – chiming the measure of our days…

In the Port on Vasilyevsky Island a rusty horse-tram crawls along. The shabby horses with their bald patches and sharp tailbones might be pulling a funeral bier, a rusty catafalque-tram. On top the corpse-passengers sway, knocking their bony shoulders one against the other. The wind from the Neva sweeps around their heads.

The rattling tram has crawled by…

On the Nikolayev Bridge the wind has piled up crumbly snow. Hissing, the snow whirled around feet, blew in faces. Petrov clutched his hat, as the fringes of his coat flapped: "Let the wind wail…"

He touched a bronze horse's head on the railing, ran his hand over the horse's arched neck, and onto a bronze triton, muttering,

"Who built this railing? I can't remember anymore… Thomon built it, no, not Thomon – Montferrand… It's all the same… They take it all down – the railings, the squares, Peter the Great…"

He breathed in the icy air, the noisy darkness.

"Thomon, Montferrand, Quarenghi, the Voronikhins, Rastrelli – hey! GarbIncin took down the granite, the palaces, the Kazan Cathedral, its hundred and thirty columns, with all its banners,

Marshal Davout's baton, Kutuzov's tomb![2] It has stripped everything – it has robbed all Russia! Listen! Hey!"

And suddenly an icy breeze rushed over his face, wailing hollowly with the sound of a thousand voices:

"We hear you…"

The pale passersby and the destitute on the streets of the Commune glanced fearfully around. All of them had jutting cheekbones; their emaciated faces shone with a pure light, like white snow…

The people of the Commune walk in a gloomy dream. A woman wrapped up in scarves, wearing men's boots, drags a sledge loaded with bags. The woman was panting hoarsely, lifting a burning eye, perhaps because the rope for the sledge was crushing her breast, or out of pity at the sight of a man running without a hat on in the fierce cold… Petrov has collapsed against the railing of the Summer Gardens. Dark throngs of trees rustle beyond the hoar-frosted railing. A wintry storm-cloud, like a massive black wing, has settled over the radio tower beside the Engineers' Castle.

A black wing has frozen over the capital, over Russia, over the whole earth…

And suddenly a silvery sound poured out over the murky twilight with its lingering chime: "How Glorious Is Our Lord…"

The chiming of "How Glorious Is Our Lord" poured from the railings of the Summer Gardens, from the naked trees, from the colonnades beyond the white wilderness of the Field of Mars,

---

2. Jean-François Thomas de Thomon, Auguste de Montferrand, Giacomo Quarenghi, Andrei and his nephew Nikolai Voronikhin, and Francesco Rastrelli were neoclassical architects who designed major buildings in Saint Petersburg and Moscow during the eighteenth and early nineteenth centuries. The Kazan Cathedral in central Saint Petersburg, completed by Andrei Voronikhin in 1811, has a total of 136 columns; the following year, spoils captured from Napoleon's defeated Grande Armée, including the baton (or symbol of office) of the French general Marshal Davout, were stored there. Field Marshal Kutuzov, instrumental in the French defeat, was later buried in the cathedral.

from the old house by the abutment of the Trinity Bridge, from the monument to General Suvorov, a frozen Roman warrior with his marble shield protecting the tiara of the popes and the crowns of the Italian kings, from the embankments, from the dead silvery hulk of Saint Petersburg – a silvery chiming rung from the granite pavements, from the lightless palaces…

Plunging into the drifts, Petrov runs hatless the length of the railing of Rumyantsev Square.

GarbIncin… The dark courtyard of a state building… At the farthest entrance, a dim lantern glimmers, as if outside a mortuary.

All of Saint Petersburg is chiming, all its darkness, the hollow wind, the slantwise tumbling snow: "How Glorious Is Our Lord…"

Snowy fog gusted under the arches. Petrov took a step and fell against the frozen doorpost: the chiming storm sighed into his face.

The eyes of the emperors and empresses sparkle and chime, the iron cheeks of the generals chime and shake, their soldered lips are chiming… On Catherine's marble shoulder, a chiming eagle beats a wing. The eagle's plumage rattles and flickers.

The empress crisscrossed with obscene inscriptions benevolently extends her battered fingers, her hacked cheek (gnawed by a silver wolf-cub) quivers with a chiming smile…

The bronze of the Emperor Nicholas' horse thunders. The bulging-browed iron head – Field Marshal Kutuzov's, with the hole in its back – rolled off and bounced. The iron mouth split with a chiming howl.

The eagles on the sharp-edged scraps of shredded porphyry, bending the stumps of their wings, clawing at their plinths, clattering their iron plumes, flung themselves at him in a flock, seizing him in their chiming talons…

High soar the eagles, scattering the frozen gloom with their wings…

And he sees: translucent hordes flying with the eagles; translucent generals with epaulettes of ice; children more translucent than moon-smoke, and among them N, N, N; and overtaking the children, translucent people, naked, riddled with wounds, with dark patches on their brows, on their breasts, with black bullet-holes; old women, frozen from hunger and more translucent than icicles, fly in a whirling dance; translucent cavalcades, translucent Saint Petersburg…

The bells of the fortress, pouring forth their icy vibration, ring out the quarter-hour in the emptiness of the dark sky, as Petrov, manager of the GarbIncin storeroom, knocks out the window-frame and tumbles from the sixth floor into the courtyard…

He was removed the following day. The Comrade Secretary of the Communal Housing Commission, inspecting the district, chanced to wander into the deserted court.

For a long time the Comrade Secretary studied the objects poking out of a snowdrift, before bending down and noticing that they were a pair of legs in Triangle-brand rubber boots, held together with string. The heels had been completely worn away…

1925

THE VENETIAN MIRROR

Pavel Muratov

I broke my promise; I never did send you a Venetian mirror –
one of those Venetian mirrors that we admired so much among the
patricians' palaces, the hucksters' stalls, and the deserted villas on the
banks of the Brenta. Your eyes will never be reflected in that glass,
streaked with enamel and silver.

Nor will the marvelously ornate curves of the gilded frame on the
wall of your room in the village ever encircle the fragments of its
magical world. Even now I can see that room. The window stands
open on the spangled glints of a summer's day. The shadow of a
bird slips across the green glade as it sails silently through the sky.
Eternally idle, the Sèvres shepherdess never tires of her sparkling
white reflection on the polished wood of the side table. A wasp
drones, feebly bumping its small body against the faded wallpaper,
lured by the fragrance of apples.

I know your apple orchard and the ring of aged elms by the terrace,
where squirrels springing from branch to branch love to make their
nests. Barely will the train have flashed through Eidkunen, near the
Prussian border, rumbling in its night flight across the bridges of
Russian rivers, than I will imagine glimpsing your house, grown dark
with age. I will hear the clatter of carriage wheels over the little log
bridge joining your avenue to the main road. Running straight as an
arrow from the station, the road disappears into the rural distance.
The clouds will be soft-edged, the fragrances damp. The sun, sinking

westwards, will be quenched in the mist rising from the nearby marshes. The darkening woods will fill with echoes and fresh scents. Wild ducks will fly low overhead, wings beating heavily. On the slope above the little brook, gray rocks show bare through the earth. The glow of the Northern sunset will spill across the sky, barely coloring the dim surfaces of the deep lakes.

Do these unruffled lakes of yours recall to your mind the expanse of the lagoon, which you glimpsed for the last time through a train window? I remember the day of your departure. How troubled and serious our two *barcaioli* appeared to me as they slowly propelled the Venetian boat through the narrow canals. The side of our gondola briefly struck against the gray stone of the Palazzo Grimani, and we found ourselves for an instant confronted with the reflection of the Canal Grande, trembling upon the waters. You turned towards the Rialto: the tiny figures, dawdling on the stone slabs of the bridge, seemed to you already far-off and spectral in their unfeigned gaiety. Completing a half-circle, the gondola curved around a red house before plunging into the Rio San Paolo. The narrow sliver of sky above our heads stretched out before us, the rowers plied their oars by turns, with concentration. We were both silent, listening to their drawn-out hails. A little dog, barking at us from a coalman's barge that brushed past our boat, made you laugh. I saw the merriment on your face before we were swallowed in the suddenly approaching shadow of a bridge. Involuntarily we glanced up; a girl in a black shawl, identical to one we had bought together on the Rialto, was running up the steps of the arch that spanned the banks. She stopped short and made us a small sign with her hand. Her agate eye shone with a wily Venetian farewell. An instant later we heard the patter of her sandals, moving away.

Like many others before you and like many after, you were borne away by a train rumbling over the long iron bridge to Mestre. As the rails were revealed in all their undeviating rigidity, I was left alone in the crowd of porters as they donned again the caps they had doffed in the moment of farewell. Amid these decent folk, busy with their labors, I left the Venetian railway station and directed my steps to the vaporetto quay.

I disembarked in the narrow Strada Ridotto. I had not forgotten the promise I gave you. How often we made this journey together! I peered through the corner pane of a shop window at the old wines darkening in their dusty bottles, their labels still commanding respect. On the Strada San Moisè, the foreign visitors thronging under the roof of Bauer's Hotel de Ville were lingering as usual in front of Alinari's shop windows and the souvenir vendors. The Baroque church with its lavish reliefs, scrolled pediments, and carvings of saints, struck you as a mere trinket that a covetous giant might have seized for his cabinet of curiosities! I passed by a dull street and crossed a bridge. Here, between two bridges set almost side by side, I leaned down and peered into the window below.

You surely haven't forgotten our friend Gennaro Pasquale? I could see his artfully uncombed head level with my knees. The goldsmith and decorator wiped his hand on his apron before offering it to me. Unhurriedly, we discussed the object of my quest. The Venetian lit up a cigarillo, carefully moving aside a bottle of lacquer. I liked the air of his workshop, which mingled odors of powerful chemicals, dyes, and wood chips. All around I saw chairs and tables, frames and candelabras, which over the centuries had shed some of their ancient gilding. Mirrors of many sorts enticed me. My pleas grew insistent. Wishing to help me, Gennaro Pasquale wrinkled his brow effortfully, twirling a long, satiny wood-shaving in his hands. Suddenly his face lit up with cunning. He slapped his palm on the white tabletop so forcefully that a weak answering chime rang out from the crystal pendants of the chandeliers awaiting his attention.

I left the workshop between the two bridges, bearing in my pocket an address scrawled in the hand of Signor Pasquale. If only briefly, I had puzzled the goldsmith, but I had never thought he could be foxed for long. Gennaro Pasquale had only allowed himself the satisfaction of teasing me with his helplessness for a few minutes. It was true that the task I had posed him was not an easy one. I desired not only to obtain an antique mirror, but I wanted the glass to be without the tiniest flaws and for the frame to be intricately carved by an especially skilled hand. I would not be satisfied by an abundance of replicated scrollwork nor by the intricacies of woodworked seashells, garlands or pine cones. I was not to be appeased by a frame with candleholders in the shape of tiny lyres, bearing witness to its former owner's musical tastes. I dreamed of a relief rich in Venice's marine and Eastern heritage: of supple, twin-tailed dolphins, of seahorses with slender bodies and tangled manes, of the prows of galleys and the heads of little Arabian children, their cheeks puffed and gilded eyes open wide in eternal astonishment.

Without any difficulty, I followed his directions to the dwelling of Signora Moricci. On the Campo Sant'Angelo, a brightly polished copper plaque still indicated the office of her late husband, a lawyer. I had been warned of the widow's somewhat unhealthy veneration for her spouse's memory. Nothing had prepared me, however, for the treasure-trove awaiting me, neither on the modest stair of this ordinary Venetian house, nor in the office itself, to which a little servant girl admitted me. Everything here had been left exactly as if the lawyer had only just seen his latest client. I observed dull Viennese furniture, paisley divans, a desk with a pile of papers, an inkwell full of ink, a quill ready for use and different-colored sands for blotting. Garibaldi and Cavour looked down splendidly from the walls, and a black-bordered portrait with a metal palm frond depicted the lawyer Moricci in his ceremonial redingote, long-faced, with side whiskers in the style of King Vittorio Emmanuel.

The mistress of the house entered the room, and I bowed to her: an old lady in widow's weeds, with a lively, pleasant look. We sat down. "I know what has brought you here," said Signora Moricci, and added with a gentle sigh, "What am I to do? In my circumstances, certain things become luxuries; I have decided to part with all the rest, so as to keep only these untouched." The lawyer's widow glanced around the office. "Would you like to take a look?" she abruptly recollected herself, rising; I followed her. Unexpectedly for me, the old lady pulled aside a drape concealing, as I guessed, a door. This opened onto a small study, filled with shabby seventeenth-century furniture. Perhaps on this sofa, upholstered in flower-scattered satin, the lawyer had received beautiful lady clients seeking divorces? Before me, I saw an antique mirror, somnolent, opaque, and full of shadows. How simple and artless the slender gilded frame seemed to me, encircling its marvelous oval outline! Perceiving my astonishment, the widow Moricci invited me to be seated, and began her tale.

"If you are seeking an old mirror, Signor," she said, "you will not find another more remarkable than this, although its size is not large, and its frame lacks almost any kind of embellishment. Gennaro Pasquale did not deceive you, but nor did he explain to you certain things that must be made clear. I am old, but I am not superstitious; I tend to regard things with a calm and sober eye. Thinking over this looking glass, into which I have not gazed for several years now, I believe that I have solved its strange mystery. It was made in the days when people were more sensitive and skillful. They knew the secret of compelling a precious glass to reflect the human face not as others see it, or as it is reflected in ordinary mirrors. Looking into this one, we do not see our everyday selves. You are probably an artist or an admirer of ancient paintings, and therefore I do not need to explain to you how a face can be changed by the depth of a shadow, the hue of skin, or the glitter of a pupil. Our mask of indifference suddenly slips, we live our lives to the full in a single glance. We feel love or hate, rejoicing or despair. A smile of gladness or a sneer of disappointment crooks the corners of our lips. We are left face to face with our fate, written on our features in letters that may not be erased. We recognize the past and see with our own eyes things that occurred long ago. Oh, the enchanted glass is like a miniature theatre, on whose stage we – pierced by heartache – recognize all the characters from the comedy or the drama in which we once acted! It has all happened already, but we suffer no less for knowing that, the poison of memory is no less strong..."

I stared in amazement at the Venetian lady, who appeared to have forgotten my presence as she turned sharply towards the dusty sparkle of the mirror gleaming on the wall. She went on. "Although I bear this modest name, although I became the bride of Lawyer Moricci, and my maiden name was merely Graziani, I belong to a famous Venetian family: my grandmother was one of the ancient Angaran family, and from her mother she inherited this mirror and these other things. If you are a scholar, if you spend days in the archives of San Marco, you will find testimonies there that Elisabetta Angaran was a virtuous woman, a faithful spouse, such as were not so rare in old Venice, much slandered in our times. My great-grandmother, however, was no better and no worse than others, and the custom demanded that she too have a *faithful cavaliere* of her own. Her innocent connection with Angelo Gritti, blameworthy only in the eyes of our ridiculous generation, lasted for three years.

Cavaliere Gritti was too honest and too intelligent not to be aware of the moment when the selfless tribute that men paid to Beauty became a heavy burden on his heart. Simple good manners and easy friendship made way within him for more profound and foreboding feelings. Angelo Gritti intended unhesitatingly to fulfil his duty: he requested that the Republic send him to Brescia. On the day of his departure he sat in Elisabetta Angaran's small salon, with hanging head, gripping his cane with cold fingers, his three-cornered hat dropped on the carpet. My great-grandmother had turned her back; she was gazing out the window, restraining unshed tears. The words of farewell were uttered. Angelo Gritti rose to kiss the small, trembling hand and execute a last, low, and formal bow. As he rose from his chair, his distracted glance swept the walls. His eye paused on this glass. Gritti shuddered and approached the mirror, as if drawn magnetically.

When he turned towards Elisabetta, his face was inspired and dreadful. Terrified, she covered her face with both hands. Angelo Gritti took a purposeful step towards her. Tenderly and firmly, he drew her little hands away. Bowing his head to Elisabetta Angaran, he kissed her on the lips…" With rising agitation, Signora Moricci made an effort to continue her tale. "Angelo Gritti never left," she cried. "If, in the archives of San Marco, you find Elisabetta Angaran's name, do not trust it again. She tasted the sweetness of a single betrayal, only to learn the torments of many more. Cavaliere Gritti died a violent death, the specter of which he saw – together with the mirage of love – for the first time in this glass." The Venetian lady rose from her seat and pointed at the mirror. I barely heard her words; a strange temptation had mastered me. Signora Moricci was almost whispering in my ear. "The mirror's powers have been proven by others; they have been tested many times. In my own life, in my quiet life as the wife of one of the worthiest men in Venice, I have tried it." Following my interlocutor's example, I rose from the sofa. I stepped forwards and stared greedily into the depths of the mirror. My heart skipped, as though a powerful hand had gripped it; I cried out.

I ran from Signora Moricci's house, like one trying to outrace mortal danger. I could not outrace myself. On the streets and squares of Venice I vainly called your name. I cursed the day of your decision and the hour of your departure. Thousands of plans, impossible for me now, sprang up in my mind. I seized on ragged scraps of hope, wove together threads lost long ago. The tattered garments of submission fell from me; I flung away contemptuously the mask of magnanimity I had assumed. The beautiful city seemed to me a prison, onto whose stone floor I had been heartlessly flung. The heavens and the waters reflected in their vastness the face of despair and passion that I saw in the Venetian glass, streaked with enamel and silver…

I write to you after rousing from my oppressive trance of these last days. I am now, once again, the man I was when I watched your train disappear into the distance, or when, searching for a Venetian mirror, I described Signora Moricci's home as our friend Gennaro Pasquale had described it to me. But would it surprise you that I have not followed my quest to its promised end? There is no glass I can consider worthy of you after that mirror full of hidden power, which I saw slumbering mysteriously on the wall as I listened to the tale of Elisabetta Angaran and Angelo Gritti. I have tried that power and I do not wish the same trial upon you. Perhaps Signora Moricci, alarmed by her foreign visitor's yell and his flight, will shatter her enchanted glass. May the passionate face imprisoned within it, the frenzied voice, never seduce our hearts. May the marvelous gilded frame never hang on that wall, spangled with the glints of summer, in the peace of your room in the countryside, to encircle the fragments of its magical world.

1922

THE COMPANION

Pavel Muratov

Entire books could be written about the oddities of Lord Elmore. As a youth, he hearkened to the flights of elves and fairies amid the eternally mist-shrouded groves of his ancestral Woburn Abbey. In the visions that came to him then, there appeared mostly Eastern djinns and peris; the dreadful Ifrit once destroyed his slumbers, fearing however to cross the enchanted circle inscribed around his bed. The morning after these nocturnal horrors young Lord Elmore would rest in his beloved pavilion in his park. Leaning against a column, he would compose obscure, melancholy verses or toy with the strings of his little harp.

He was wealthy beyond belief, and uncommonly handsome. He owned entire tropical islands with tobacco and sugar plantations, and whole towns in old England, with gray Gothic cathedrals and miserable terraces of sooty chimneys. His appearance was striking; a rare harmony distinguished his features. The softness of his cheeks complemented the pride of his high forehead and the delicacy of his well-shaped nose. His deep-blue eyes had a gift for sometimes glowing as transparently as the sky, sometimes flashing with dark fire. His golden locks coiled in wide, natural waves. His figure, and the straightness of its lines, were worthy of any Apollo from ancient Greece. Lord Elmore was well aware of this, and indeed it even inspired a daring prank that somewhat contradicted the loftiness of his youthful fancies and his reserved way of life.

Clearly youth will have its way, for the young lord yielded on one occasion to the insistence of his peers and joined in their daring antics. When, during a formal reception in the Abbey, the door of the gallery of statues was opened wide, the noble guests, much astonished, saw not a classical deity imported from Italy, but the real Elmore on a pedestal, assuming the traditional archer's pose, his complete nudity barely covered by a flimsy girdle. The elderly ladies swooned away, while a certain ruddy country squire could not suppress a belly-laugh. All was confusion; the scene threatened to become all too memorable. In view of this, conceding to his elders' urgings, the young lord left hurriedly for the continent.

Lord Elmore travelled. He was accompanied by a German professor, who acted as his mentor and taught him the principles of philosophy, competing with the Italian *maestro* who developed his musical talent. The young dreamer and spirit-seer, as he set foot on foreign shores, was suddenly consumed by thirst for all curious things, and by fever for all kinds of action. Lord Elmore rushed to fling himself headfirst into diverse life experiences. He could not be satisfied with listening to oratorios and fugues; he grew calm only when, incognito, he played the organist's part in the orchestra of the Rhenish Margrave. Drawn to the theatre, he promptly horrified his tutor by joining a troupe of wandering actors, where he played both brooding murderers and tender lovers, to acclaim. Considerable effort was later required to prevent him from entering a Trappist order and voluntarily confining himself to a monastery.

Easiest of all to Lord Elmore came luck with cards and the love of women. But pleasure never appealed to him unless combined with danger. The celebrated Venetian courtesan saw him as another indifferent client until he had the strange thought of working as her doorman. With British boldness, Lord Elmore knocked her drunken guests down the stairs, careless – in the heat of fisticuffs – of receiving a treacherous stab from a dagger or the contemptuous sting of a sword. When such feats palled for him, he boarded a boat and went East. He had long since worn out his original companions – the philosopher fell ill from constant anxiety over him, and the musician lost his memory from all the wine they had quaffed together.

Only a French servant accompanied him. Where this man had come from, no one knew; but he would never again be parted from Lord Elmore.

Auguste possessed exceptionally useful knowledge and multifarious indispensable abilities. He could be a valet, a housemaid, a stable-lad, a cook, a confidant in love, and an ally in battle. His round, eyebrowless face could mimic like an Italian harlequin or mug like an English clown. He looked so serious that a single glance at him made you want to die laughing; he was so taciturn that he would have driven a dumb man to chatter. Lord Elmore desired no better companion. He thought out loud in front of his servant, unless he addressed him directly in the language of signs. Auguste accepted blows from his master's cane and spurns from his foot, passing them on to others at once. He paid eagerly for all his mistakes, certain that he could derive profit or satisfaction from them.

However, these mistakes were few. There was no situation that could baffle the Frenchman. He always had two or three ready solutions up his sleeve; all Lord Elmore had to do was choose between them. Auguste knew everyone's affairs and social position. Neither wealth nor poverty, country nor city, honesty nor roguery held any secrets for him. He knew to perfection how to manage jealous husbands and greedy loan sharks. He felt as much at home on the parquet of a palace as on the mud floor of a hut. Without knowing a single language, he conversed so fluently that folk from all sorts of countries began feeling ignorant of their own native tongue. The folk of the East esteemed him as highly as they did his master. Thanks to his stalwart efforts, Lord Elmore had at his disposal a seraglio worthy of the sultan himself, in which he passed several months of happy leisure and utter idleness.

Suddenly, Lord Elmore drove away his fair captives and returned to Europe. Evidently his taste of polygamy had convinced him that a man needs only one wife. It was easy for the rich and handsome lord to make his choice. His wealth, in spite of all the extravagance of a Scheherazade, had not decreased; indeed it had multiplied with the years. His appearance had gained new qualities. Young Elmore had grown in manliness and strength; the Eastern sun had lightly burned his skin and bronzed the waves of his hair. His eyes, accustomed to seeing boundless seas and endless deserts, saw acutely and clearly. His step had the firmness that travelers and sailors acquire.

On the shores of Lake Geneva, Lord Elmore met his future wife, Helen. She kept her violet eyes turned to the snowy peaks of the Alps or the calm surface of the waters, raising them to the man seeking her hand only at the decisive moment of avowal. A faint blush flooded her cheeks; her heart suddenly ached, as if she had flung herself from a precipice.

Lady Helen was a gentle, simple soul; and she was very lovely. Lord Elmore proved to be an all too appreciative husband for her. He arrayed her in fine garments and showered her with precious gifts. They spent the London season in unheard-of, unnatural, alarming splendor. Inside the Elmores' home, one festive occasion followed another, vying to pass the boundaries of common sense. Their life had lost any likeness of actual reality; it dissolved among the illusions of a theatrical spectacle. Lady Helen was obliged to cast herself now as the Queen of the Fairies, now Ophelia, now Cleopatra, yet only succeeded in yearning for the simplicity and modesty of her maiden existence not long before. Elmore would surround her with a fairytale retinue, chosen from among his hangers-on, then whisk her off to the banks of the Clyde, where he would compel them both to act the parts of a miller and the miller's wife in an ivy-covered windmill – a no less artificial idyll.

Lady Helen grew into a woman, sighing, weeping secretly and dreaming of consolation. Meeting a friend from her childhood years, she opened her heart to him, and from that day on he became her secret Sorrowful Knight. On a very few occasions she sang for him songs from their shared childhood, accompanying herself with an uncertain hand. In one of those moments Lord Elmore happened to pass through the next chamber, too lost in thought to heed the music beyond the closed door. Auguste suddenly rose up beside this door with an indescribable expression on his clean-shaven face and a nearly imperceptible gesture of his hands, held respectfully by his sides. Lord Elmore shuddered, pushed open the door, and entered Lady Helen's salon.

He saw the Sorrowful Knight, bowing to kiss the little fingers as they dawdled inattentively over the black and white keyboard. Lord Elmore uttered a loud peal of mirth. An instant later he exited Lady Helen's salon, slamming the door behind him. He continued guffawing, crossing the great hall and climbing the staircase to his own apartment. Only among the dark mirrors in his room did he fall silent, as if struck by the sight of his own reflection, of his features twisted by rage.

From then on, Lord Elmore always laughed, loudly and unrestrainedly, as soon as he saw Lady Helen. She never stopped hearing this horrible laughter, even when she was alone. Seated in her chamber, she stopped her ears to no effect; and, flinging herself on her bed, vainly covered herself with pillows. Her weak mind began betraying signs of obvious disturbance; she fell ill. Her spouse had her brought to Woburn Abbey; he ceased to trouble her with his visits, leaving her to the care of doctors and female relations. In her illness, Lady Helen lost her memory, which aided her recovery. She began rising from her bed again; she was taken out for strolls in the park. No one knew where Lord Elmore might be found, and no one mentioned him in her presence.

Once she was returning from a stroll around sundown. An elderly lady had taken her arm while her devoted maid rolled a bath chair just behind, leaving the track of its two wheels on the damp sand of the avenue. A servant was waiting for her on the terrace; but not the old valet she had brought with her from her parents' house. Auguste swept her a low and respectful bow. She stopped short in confused anxiety. The Frenchman raised his head; his thin mouth stretched wide to form a noiseless laugh, summoning in Helen's heart the echoes of that thunderous, hellish guffaw. She gave a shriek, and fainted.

Lady Helen never recovered; she died; and Lord Elmore had no wish to attend her funeral. He racketed through Europe, scattering money, leaving behind a trail of japes and frenzies. Tales were told of his monstrous orgies; they credited him with a whole list of crimes. In Paris he sought out a young actress with a look of Lady Helen; he tricked her out as Ophelia and sat at her feet, like the Danish prince, while her fellow actors played before them, in his domestic theatre, scenes from his diseased imagination. Lord Elmore wept tears that were sometimes real and sometimes drunken; he showered his current favorite with entreaties worthy of angels one moment and crude vulgarities the next.

His whims soon exceeded the bounds of private life. He shifted the vanity of his illusions, and his games of mimicry, to re-enacting historical events. He kitted out a vessel and sailed the seas like a modern-day corsair, brazenly violating laws and customs. This frolic would not have turned out well for him had he not taken care to ensure a happy ending for his piratical deeds. He forced the passengers of the ship he had lately captured to walk the plank so he could chuckle over them flailing in the water; in the end, they were rescued by his own vessels. A merchant robbed at sea by Elmore would unfailingly receive, once he got home, a cheque that precisely compensated his loss; and a maiden deprived in his cabin of her greatest treasure would be rewarded with a round sum guaranteeing her a happy marriage.

Next Lord Elmore bought land in Africa and turned himself into a little emperor. He kept ministers and diplomats, coined money, equipped an army. He entered upon diplomatic relations, jesting and ceremonial, with his neighbors, the black kings; he sent them ambassadors and gifts, exchanging Manchester calicos and Sheffield blades for ostrich feathers and elephant tusks. He declared war, attained victories and suffered defeats. In the evenings he withdrew to his rattan-lined room in his straw palace. By the light of a tallow candle, he drank rum straight from the bottle to the health of his royal African brothers. Auguste served him silently; black shadows rushed across the walls when Lord Elmore bounded up and, turning to his ever-constant companion, tried to express in grimaces the stately buffoonery of the day just passed. Once, maddened by his own shadow, he set it on fire with a candle. The straw palace blazed up; Elmore barely managed to escape, singeing his hair and eyebrows.

Unsatisfied, he fetched up in England. After the submissiveness of his black subjects, he missed the rebellious natures of his compatriots. He settled on one of his estates and, having been indifferent until then to the fate of his peasants, he now deliberately took to weighing them down with taxes and extortionate fees. By his orders, brutal stewards used every means to exhaust the patience of the long-suffering farmers. He hired agitators to skillfully sow the seeds of discontent and rebellion everywhere. Lord Elmore hearkened with joy to the tumult swelling steadily around him. Eventually there was an uprising. Standing on the belvedere of his house, Elmore watched the red blaze of arson and heard the furious hubbub of peasant revolution. A crowd of peasants, armed with pitchforks and shotguns, burst onto his property, wrecking everything in their path. Satisfied with such a perfectly staged performance, Lord Elmore calmly slipped away under the very noses of the rebels, dressed as an old crone. After returning to the capital, he ordered that all the fines extracted from the peasants be returned to them, and that their land be restored without punishment. With these orders he also sent a bag of gold coins, commanding that each of the performers in his spectacle receive one.

Years passed; Lord Elmore grew old. Those who remembered him posing as Apollo come to life on the pedestal of a classical statue would no longer have known him. Fine wrinkles netted his face, which had taken on a yellow parchment hue. His nose and chin sharpened; his fingers withered and seemed longer than ever. Only his eyes retained the strangely youthful expression of before; now cerulean blue, now dark and flashing fire. Nor had Lord Elmore lost his agility or the hidden strength of his movements. The earth, as always, bore him lightly, ready to engrave on her many different surfaces the zigzags of his whimsical wanderings.

These wanderings ended abruptly. Lord Elmore shut himself away in his ancestral Woburn Abbey. For many months he could be seen out either walking, leaning on a cane, or mounted, gazing at the construction of the exceedingly long stone wall with which he had resolved to enclose his property. Thousands of stonemasons labored on it; the wall climbed over hills and descended into valleys, cutting through tillage, girdling woodlands. Whole villages falling within its circle were dismantled at the master's command and rebuilt in a different location. Arrogant with his equals, Elmore was sympathetic and generous to common folk. On several occasions he joined the laborers at their modest breakfast, smoked a pipe with them and shared a few swigs of beer. Growing thoughtful, he told them tales of his travels, and they considered him a good-hearted and garrulous master.

Those were his final conversations with others. His unexpected garrulity ended with the construction of the wall. From that day on, Lord Elmore never crossed over its boundary. A few servants, stablehands, a cook and a groom now made up the entire population of his estate, fenced in by that impassable barrier. Auguste managed the house; no one now oversaw either the park, doomed to become a wilderness, or the fields, given over to nature.

Lord Elmore plunged passionately into reading the books from his ancient library. Soon he came to regard its contents as insufficient. By his orders, heaps of ever newer volumes began appearing at Woburn. The shelves were over-filled; books no longer fitted on the walls of the library and spread into the connecting rooms, spilling in disorder across the tables and the floor. Lord Elmore devoured them with unusual, feverish speed. His lamp burned long after midnight, the only light amid the dark stone masses of the Abbey. Struck by some thought, he would straighten his back and bound to his feet. One hand would seize the candle in its holder, the other would clutch the skirts of his gown. Shuffling his slippers, Elmore would descend the stairs into the suite of rooms crammed with books. He would search, crossing from one pile to another, unlocking cupboards, clambering up stepladders. The flame of his candle, placed on a leather folio, trembled; his hands leafed unceasingly through pages; his nail deeply underscored a certain line. A deadly cold penetrated Lord Elmore's heart, and a tormenting sweat broke out on his forehead. Flinging his book aside, he would stand listening for a long time, hearkening to the soft noises of scampering mice and the nameless sounds of the night.

In the morning, breathing in fresh air, he would gallop out across the neglected meadows of his estate, accompanied by the groom. In spite of his age and the nights and days now spent among dusty books, he felt strong and bold. Woburn never saw a doctor within its walls. Its owner lightly leaped fences, guiding his favorite mare, Jessica, with a confident hand. The vixens, who were thriving within the boundary wall, lured him into galloping furiously. Following them, he allowed his horse to race at full speed, risking breaking his neck at any moment, glancing back at the groom lagging far behind.

Abruptly, as ever in his life, he acquired a passion for collecting. Having chanced to wander into his gallery of paintings and statues, he had surveyed its walls with a casual glance. The very next day his orders had flown off to the ends of the earth. Lord Elmore spared no expense; obedient to his persuasive gold, sea captains pitilessly hewed down pediments on Greek islands and mule-drivers bore off masterpieces, greedily torn from the altars of a Spanish monastery. The antiquarian dealers of London and Paris sent him their rarest and most expensive items. Soon Woburn Abbey exceeded all the treasure-chambers of kings and bankers, and its fame was all the greater because not a single mortal was allowed to visit Lord Elmore's collection. He replied to all the requests he received with either a polite refusal or contemptuous silence. No small number of over-insistent visitors were obliged to retreat smartly, tails between their legs, from the very gates of the celebrated boundary wall. One journalist and art critic, who had secretly attempted to climb across it, received as punishment for his audacity a whole barrel of shot in his backside.

Neither books nor pictures taught Lord Elmore peace of mind. Can the wisdom of others calm the heart of one who has never found peace through his own experiences? The hermit of Woburn was a stranger to humility. When he should have meditated, he fulminated. He demanded immediate and precise answers to everything, as if the philosopher or scholar who wrote the book had been the skipper of Elmore's ship or one of his dark-skinned ministers. Knowledge irritated Elmore because it was incomplete, and faith annoyed him by its doubts. He learned to despise both; it was then he decided to remake everything designed by mankind from beginning to end. He developed his own systems of astronomy and mathematics. He wrote anew a complete history of nations and kingdoms, convinced that real history was entirely mistaken. Finally, Elmore conceived of God in his own image and likeness, and then, bursting with diabolical pride, he ceased to read.

His passion for paintings deserted him under different circumstances. Once he was returning from hunting vixens feeling unusually tired. It was a foggy day at the end of October. The wind, which had risen at noon, was chasing pale phantoms made of autumn mist across the wet park. Lord Elmore dismounted and walked down the sandy avenue, towards the lawn where Auguste waited for him, bowing respectfully. The servant raised his head; his face, turned towards the treetops of the park, expressed horror. The lord glanced around. Over the green pond, a cloud in the shape of a human figure floated: Elmore recognized the features of Lady Helen. One foggy arm extended and lengthened endlessly, twining around the stone redoubts of the Abbey. The hem of her cloudy robe shrouded the tops of the walls. The vision dissolved, uttering a sigh like the groan of an Aeolian harp. Lord Elmore shuddered from head to foot and hastened into the house. Seeking oblivion, he made his way hurriedly into the picture gallery. He no longer recognized its walls. He was shocked by the multiplicity of ladies, goddesses and angels gazing at him from within their golden frames. In all of them he now saw a resemblance to Lady Helen. Some smiled the same way, while others wept with her expression. Everywhere he saw her eyes, her hair, her shoulders, her hands. Her presence was confirmed, embodied, and multiplied. Lord Elmore felt panicky terror. He dashed right out of the gallery and fixed a heavy lock on its doors.

Most of the servants had left him long ago; soon the last of them departed, except Auguste. This pleased the master of Woburn. Surely the Frenchman alone could replace all the others in their many services? He changed bedlinen, cooked, cared for the horse, and rode with him like a groom. He was just as silent and just as skillful as he had ever been. He was the same eternal, wordless companion.

Auguste settled into the spacious kitchen, its walls glittering with copper and aluminum cooking-pots. Elmore now came down there to breakfast and lunch at the heavy oak table. In the evenings, he took his chair at the vast, blazing hearth and seated the Frenchman before him on a low bench. Lord Elmore drank glass after glass of wine from a dark bottle and told stories, addressing his companion. He explained to him the secrets of his discoveries and the temerity of his speculations. Auguste appeared to smile with his toothless mouth. He sat unmoving, with half-shut eyes and hands on his knees. It was impossible to tell whether he was alive or dead, asleep or alert. Elmore sometimes vainly raised his voice and furiously waved his long fingers under the other's nose. The lord would suddenly raise his hand to strike his servant, but then he caught himself, dropped his hand like a whiplash and, after drinking off the last drops in the bottle, would go staggering to bed.

Once he was telling stories about his efforts to penetrate the mystery of the Devil. Stirred up by the importance of his own words, he tippled more than ever from his glass. Everything flickered and danced before his eyes, like the tongues of flame leaping furiously in the vast hearth. Auguste, sitting still on his low bench, seemed to be swaying in a bawdy saraband. Wishing to hold him still, Lord Elmore seized him by the elbow and pulled him to his feet. The old man slid downwards like a lifeless body. This apparent resistance was enough to infuriate Elmore. With a nudge of his foot, he thrust his companion into the fire.

With insane enjoyment, he watched the flame, raging in the centuries-old hearth, devour its prize. He sat silently for a long time, intrigued by the spectacle, then raised his eyes to the low bench, expecting to find the Frenchman there, listening to his tales as if nothing had happened. Suddenly he realized that he had lost his only listener. "I know who's behind this prank," he muttered. Cursing, he threatened the fire with his fist. A new thought flashed through his mind. Elmore bent down and lifted a coal. With a trembling hand, he sketched on the white wall a figure in a long tunic with large, round buttons. Its moonlike face recalled Auguste's, but the coal-black eyes and malignant brows on either side of the hooked nose were too dark. With the coal in his hand, Lord Elmore took a few steps backwards, well satisfied with his drawing. "Listen, you!" he shouted. The daub's features twitched; its mouth twisted in a sneer, baring fangs. Elmore wished to speak, but his tongue would not obey him. He raised a hand to wipe the coal-dust figure from the white wall. His strength deserted him; he toppled backwards onto the stone floor of the kitchen.

Lord Elmore roused from his faint the following morning. He propped himself on an elbow and glanced through the window, where the wan light of a winter's day poured in. The cold hearth was covered with an ominous pile of cinders and ashes. Elmore recalled everything; rising, he strode manfully to the wall where he had traced his sketch the evening before. Thrusting his hands in his pockets, he stared at it long and squarely, then pronounced in a tone of command: "This evening you will hear me out." As if wishing to forestall any objections, he turned away immediately and hurriedly left his new companion.

Leaving the house, he made for the stables, where he led out and saddled Jessica. He sprang into the saddle as lightly as usual. With a still-powerful hand he controlled the mare, who shuddered and snorted anxiously in the echoing avenues of the wintry park. Lord Elmore rode out onto the meadows. They were covered in white hoar-frost, black earth showing through here and there, like the coal-black lines on the white wall of the kitchen. Fancying he heard hoofbeats, Lord Elmore looked behind and recognized his companion from the night before, mounted on the groom's horse and catching up. "You're in a hurry," he muttered contemptuously. "Just you wait," he shouted, spurring Jessica to a brief gallop. The new servant did not fall behind. Without looking behind, without even seeing him, Lord Elmore, with steadily rising rage, sensed his presence behind him. He let out the reins and lifted his whip. Jessica dashed forwards. The frost-covered meadow flew to meet them. The mare outpaced a flock of birds, flying heavily in the winter's cold, but her rider never ceased to feel the nearness of his rival in the race. Lord Elmore's face now grew pale; he gasped for breath; his hand flung away the reins and dropped the whip. He knew that his pursuer would halt only in that instant when he and his horse rushed together over the precipice that had opened abruptly before them.

1922

BY THE SEA

Irina Odoyevtseva

Mrs. Roberts sat alone at a little table in the large dining room of the Atlantique boarding house. Her husband had gone to London on business. Roy, her four-year-old son, was taking breakfast upstairs with the nanny.

Mrs. Roberts felt bored. She had been here a week already, and she was tired of Biarritz. Always the same sea, the same motor-cars, the same faces.

Her table stood by an open window. Two tanned-looking women came along the footpath. They were laughing and gesturing.

"And why do they carry on like that? How silly they are, how repulsive."

Mrs. Roberts served herself a piece of fish. One could see instantly, from her cautious and elegant manner of eating, that she was an Englishwoman.

"It can't be…" a woman's voice suddenly shrieked, in Russian. "It's impossible, Misha…"

"Hush, Nina. Don't make such a row…"

Mrs. Roberts turned her head and listened.

"Russians? … Where?"

But it was impossible to make anything out in the restrained hum of conversations. Some Spaniards were seated nearby; a little further away sat a wine merchant from Bordeaux. By the wall there were some Americans; she was acquainted with them. But where were the Russians? They must be that gray-haired lady beside the young

woman and the young man at the next window. She had not seen them before.

Russians. They were Russians. Her heart began thumping loudly. Mrs. Roberts shut her eyes and saw before her the wide, white streets of Petersburg, the dirty walls of its houses, its blue frosty sky. And she watched herself, Annechka Vakurina, walking over sparkling snow, in a dark-blue fur coat belted at the waist with a sash, so slender that a gust of wind might break her in two…

Breakfast was over. Mrs. Roberts carefully folded her napkin and went into the hall to wait for the Russians.

"The gray-haired lady has to be Misha and Nina's mother," she thought.

The Russians also entered the hall.

"We should ask the porter whether the tram goes to Bayonne."

"Oh yes," Mrs. Roberts said quickly in Russian, "the tram does go to Bayonne."

The gray-haired lady smiled.

"Are you Russian? How pleased I am."

"And I am also very pleased."

They left the boarding house together.

"God has sent you to me in answer to my prayers," the gray-haired old lady was saying. "Just think how it is for me. I am alone and haven't got a soul to talk to. Nina is always with Mikhail Andreyevich. What can one do – they're engaged to be married. But now I have caught you, I won't let you go!"

Mrs. Roberts put on her gloves, thinking: that means Misha is the fiancé, and not the brother. This Misha doesn't have very good taste.

"I wouldn't dream of trying to escape," she said. "My husband is an Englishman and all our friends are English. It's been so long since I spoke Russian…"

They returned late, just before dinner.

Roy was sitting on the grass in the garden, looking serious and hitting a stone with a red spade.

Mrs. Roberts ran to him and took him in her arms. How awful. She had left her child on his own all day.

"Did you miss me, Roy my sweet?" she asked him in English.

The child shook his blond, curly head seriously.

"No, not a bit."

She burst out laughing and kissed him on the cheek.

"That's the sort of boy my son is!"

Nina cautiously stroked his springy hair.

"He's adorable. Look, Misha, what a cutie."

Mrs. Roberts smiled gratefully at her.

"Yes, he's a fine boy. God willing, you'll have one just like him soon."

"No, not just like him. He's charming, but he's a little Englishman. And ours will be all Russian."

Mrs. Roberts' eyebrows rose. She gazed coldly at Nina.

"I have still to change before dinner…" And she left for her room, carrying the child.

❋

"How fortunate you are, Nina, to be marrying a Russian…"

The green waves reared high and collapsed, shattering their white foam across the warm gray sand. Bathers hopped along, clinging to the guide rope. A bewhiskered photographer strolled by the shore. Music drifted from the casino.

They were lying on the sand. Mrs. Roberts was in the middle, with Nina on her left and Mikhail Andreyevich on her right.

"Just think: you can use the familiar *thou* in Russian. You can say: *I love thee.*"

He was staring at Mrs. Roberts' lips.

"And have you really never said those words in Russian?"

She stretched herself, exposing her white knees to the sun.

"No. Never. Only in English, and that's not the same thing at all."

"That's why you say it so wonderfully. Say it one more time, please."

"I love thee…" she said again, slowly and singsong.

Nina blushed.

"How sentimental you are. You've become quite the Englishwoman." She rose.

"Let's go for a bathe instead."

Mrs. Roberts ran into the sea and swam off at once with clean strokes.

Nina clung to the rope.

"Misha, hold on to me, I'm scared."

But he was already swimming after Mrs. Roberts.

"Hold on tighter to the rope, Nina. I'll be back in a tick."

Mrs. Roberts was lying on her back, arms outstretched, studying the hot blue sky through her eyelashes.

He swam up to her.

"Feeling good?" he asked quietly, looking her in the face.

"Very good," she answered, just as quietly, and smiled.

Mrs. Roberts was writing a letter to her husband.

"I am having a very jolly time here. I have made friends with a Russian family; they are delightful."

She grew thoughtful for a moment. Might he take offence? And she added:

"But all the same come back as soon as you can, John dear."

"Anna Nikolayevna," someone called from below.

She put her head out the window.

Mikhail Andreyevich was standing in the garden beside a bed of gillyflowers. Nina was walking up to the gate.

"And Nina said you would be asleep. Come down as quick as you can. We'll wait for you," he shouted.

"Just a moment."

She hurriedly put on her hat, powdered her nose, took a parasol. The letter to her husband was left unfinished.

In the lobby, she found Alexandra Ivanovna, Nina's mother, sitting down.

"Are you going out again? Won't you sit with me?"

"I can't, I'm going for a walk with your family."

Alexandra Ivanovna compressed her lips.

"It must be the custom in England, then, never to leave an engaged couple by themselves?"

Mrs. Roberts burst out laughing. "Oh, not at all. Quite the opposite." And she walked out into the garden.

Nina and Mikhail Andreyevich were standing by the garden gate and quarrelling, quietly.

"I'm not going with her…"

"And I'm telling you…"

Mrs. Roberts came up to them.

"Where are we off to?"

Nina shrugged her shoulders.

"Nowhere. Or wherever you want. It's all the same to me."

"Oh, please don't be a bore, Nina," he interrupted her. "We were going to go to Saint Jean-de-Luz."

"Wonderful. I haven't been there yet."

They walked out onto the street. Nina halted suddenly.

"Very well then. Go by yourselves. I'll stay home."

Mikhail Andreyevich smiled mockingly.

"As you wish, but we'll still have a good time without you. Well, what's it to be? Are you staying?"

Nina bit her lip.

"No, I'll come…"

❋

Mrs. Roberts ran up the stairs, opened the door, and turned on the light. How jolly it had been! How well he danced. And that little goose was jealous, clearly. She laughed, flung off her cape, pulled her white lace dress over her head and walked across to the mirror.

"How pretty I look today!"

The mirror reflected the bed and a vase filled with roses. A small blue rectangle lay on the red tray table beside the door.

"A telegram."

She turned quickly. Her heart was thumping loudly. Her fingers were trembling and she couldn't rip the paper; since childhood she had dreaded telegrams.

"Tomorrow. Ten a.m. John."

She sighed. Thank God. She had had such a fright. John was on his way. She must rise early, go to meet him. How happy Roy would be…

She undressed hastily.

How happy Roy would be… And she herself? Could it be she wasn't glad? No, of course she was. Very much so.

The bed was wide; so wide, that one could lie crossways. Tomorrow there would already be less room. Tomorrow John would be lying beside her. And she would have to close the shutters; John couldn't bear the moonlight.

Of course, she was very glad…

❈

Roy was clapping and leaping around a toy battleship.

"Look! Look at its cannons!"

John stooped over his suitcase.

"I brought you some lace, darling. I'll find it in a second."

"Later, later. Let's go and swim. And I'm quite sure that Roy desperately wants to launch his boat on the water as soon as possible."

On the beach, they met Mikhail Andreyevich and Nina.

"My husband," Mrs. Roberts introduced him. "He has only just arrived." Mikhail Andreyevich frowned slightly. Or had she imagined that? John, smiling, showing his shiny white teeth, shook hands firmly.

"Very pleased to make your acquaintance. How do you do?"

Mikhail Andreyevich spoke a little English. John amicably, and painstakingly, stammered out French words.

"Marvelous weather. Isn't it?"

"Yes."

"And the sea's marvelous. Isn't it?"

"Yes, of course."

"How splendid a swim will be. It was hot on the train…"

Nina wrapped her brightly colored beach robe more tightly around her.

"I'm very pleased for you, Anna Nikolayevna. Now you won't be so lonely anymore."

❋

That same evening they left to visit with the Gibbses on their estate. She was very much disinclined to go. But there was no putting it off – the Gibbses were celebrating their fifth wedding anniversary.

"I don't like to leave Roy with the nanny."

"We can take him with us, if you'll fret."

She shrugged her shoulders.

"Dragging a child with us for just two days away. Simply comical…"

The Gibbses had a wonderful property, but those three days seemed to her endless. Never in her life had she experienced such yearning and anxiety.

Mrs. Gibbs tried to insist that they stay longer.

"Thank you. But I really can't. I worry about Roy. You are a mother yourself, Mrs. Gibbs. You understand." Mrs. Gibbs' eyes became round with sympathy.

"Oh, yes. I understand you, Mrs. Roberts."

❋

At home, everything was fine. Roy, tanned and cheerful, flung himself at his father with a yell. Then he politely kissed his mother's hand.

"Hello, darling."

He was just like his father. How similar they were – as if there were two Johns! Both blue-eyed, healthy, sensible. One big, one small.

"Mama, please don't kiss me so hard. It hurts."

She pressed him to her breast.

"You'll have to bear it, my sweet Roy. What else am I to do, when I love you so?"

Roy nodded seriously: "Very well, kiss me, I'll bear it…"

When they went downstairs, Nina and her mother were already sitting at their table in the dining room. They were alone, without Mikhail Andreyevich. Nina's eyes were red.

Mrs. Roberts touched none of the food. Her anxiety had not yet passed. But what was the cause of it? Roy was well and John was beside her. What more did she need?

"You look pale, darling. Perhaps the ocean has a bad effect on you?"

"Oh not at all, I feel very well here."

"Isn't it boring for you? Go to Poire, order yourself a new dress. That will distract you."

She tried to smile.

"You're very good, John. But I'm not bored, and I have plenty of dresses."

After lunch, she went to speak to Nina.

"Hello. How do you do? Where has Mikhail Andreyevich got to?"

Nina's eyes, red from weeping, stared at her with hatred.

"How should I know? What do you want from me?"

Nina jumped out of her chair and ran into the garden.

Alexandra Ivanovna sighed gustily.

"How agitated Nina has become. You must forgive her. She's had a tiff with her fiancé. All nonsense – young lovers will quarrel…"

Nina put out the light, kicked off her slippers and, wearing just stockings, in darkness so as not to disturb her mother, never pausing, roamed from one end of the room to the other.

Had he really left her? Was it possible?

She cautiously brushed past a chair.

"Oh, what is it? What?" Alexandra Ivanovna's sleepy voice came from behind the door. "Thieves? Robbers?"

"Go to sleep, Mama, it's just me."

It was impossible... Only ten days ago he had been so much in love with her. The wedding was in a month. Why hadn't she stayed in Paris? And now, now... and it was all this Anna's doing...

"Anna," Nina whispered, with revulsion. She had always hated that name. She even disliked *Anna Karenina* because of the name. It was as if she had sensed in advance that an Anna would destroy *her* life...

She had to rest, to sleep. Oh, how dreadful she felt.

She lay down, pressing her cheek to the cold pillow. Tears leaked swiftly from her eyes.

From tiredness, and from the tears, her head grew heavy and, like a stone, she sank to the depths of sleep.

And suppose he came back tomorrow and all was well again, she thought, drifting off...

❋

"Nina, Nina, now, Nina!"

Alexandra Ivanovna was standing by the bed. Red patches glowed on her cheeks; her face was cross and worried.

"There. At last. Now, read this," thrusting a letter into Nina's hand. "Go on, read it!"

Nina bent over the thin paper, covered in familiar handwriting. What did this mean? What?

"... To my great regret... Disparity of character... A mistake... It would be criminal to make your daughter unhappy..."

So that was how it was. The page fell onto the red blanket. Nina once again laid her head on the pillow and shut her eyes. Her soul became quite peaceful... It was better like this, much better. Now, at least, everything was clear. There was neither fear nor hope...

"Why aren't you saying anything, Nina?"

"Please don't, Mama," Nina pressed her mother's hand to her breast. "Please don't, Mama, it hurts me."

"Hurting? Your heart hurts? And don't you think my heart hurts? It's a good thing your poor father isn't alive today. He couldn't have borne this disappointment..."

Nina covered her ears.

"Mama, I beg you..."

"I told you, you didn't listen. You yourself knew better. You ran after him. Well, this is where your running brought you. You had to have Biarritz; well, now you have your Biarritz. I hope you're pleased with yourself!"

Nina lay still, pressing her head into the pillow. If only she could block out the screeching, if only her mother would leave. How her heart was hurting...

"Well, are you listening or not? Get up at once, the train leaves at two. We still have to pack. Tomorrow you'll go to see Jean and you'll ask for your old place back in the workshop..."

Nina rose, washed, and went to the bathroom.

She felt neither sorrow nor grief; she could think of nothing. Everything was meaningless to her. Only her mother troubled her. Why did she screech so rudely?

She had to hurry. To pack her suitcase...

She combed her cropped locks. In the mirror her pale, sad, tear-swollen face looked slightly cross-eyed.

It was all over... Her happiness hadn't lasted for long...

She pictured Misha's flat. The dining room with a big lamp over the round table, the sunny yellow bedroom with the huge bronze bed, the respectful maidservant in a lace apron. And herself, Nina, entering the hall in the squirrel-fur coat Misha had promised her for their wedding day. She would look so pretty, so elegant, so happy...

She placed her head on the dressing-table and wept. Then she stood, opened the cupboard, groped among the medicines, and found the opium. Her mother had been prescribed it that spring. Excellent;

some of it remained. She sniffed; it smelled disgusting. She glanced in the mirror.

"I'm about to die. So young. A shame that my eyelids are red and my lips swollen from weeping. I'd rather have died looking beautiful. But it's all the same…"

She raised the glass to her mouth. No, no, she couldn't… And yet she drank it all down.

"There's the end. There's the end of everything…"

She went slowly to her bed and lay down on her back. Straightaway she felt calm and light. She closed her eyes. Somewhere quite near she could hear music…. There were rose stalks in the vase. A servant offered her a dish of chocolate ice-cream. Of course, it was the casino. Dancers circled slowly. Misha was sitting beside her. Smiling, he kissed her hand. And everything was chiming, chiming, and spinning. How pleasant it was. How light. How peaceful…

"I must tell Mama," she suddenly recalled, and, with difficulty, sat up on the bed. "I must say goodbye to Mama."

She rose heavily and, staggering, went towards the door. The handle was round and slippery. How hard that door was to open!

Alexandra Ivanovna was on her knees in front of the suitcase. She looked crossly at her daughter.

"At last! And are your things ready?… Here, take a look, what sort of bill they've given us…"

"Mama," Nina said quietly, "Mama, farewell, I've taken poison…"

She sat on a chair by the wall. Her head hung helplessly on her breast.

"Mama, farewell…"

Alexandra Ivanovna stood up quickly.

"What? What are you saying, Nina?"

Nina shook her head weakly.

The room suddenly filled up with moist white fog. And once again everything chimed and spun…

"I poisoned myself. Farewell. Call Misha…"

"Ninochka, Ninochka. For the love of God… Nina."

Alexandra Ivanovna shook her daughter by the shoulders.

But Nina no longer saw or heard anything.

"Sleep…" she whispered.

＊

Outside the windows the sky was turning gray. The trees swayed and tossed noisily. A fresh breeze was tearing at the curtains.

Mrs. Roberts placed her napkin on the table.

"Go and swim, John. I'll catch you up at the beach. I'll just change my clothes. I'm cold in this dress."

John looked at her.

"I ought to wait for you here."

She arched her brows impatiently.

"No, no. Off you go."

"Very well, darling."

He kissed his wife's cheek and went out. He was used to not quarrelling with her. Mrs. Roberts remained alone. She looked out the window at the cold, cloudy sky, the trembling leaves. Dew was still glistening on the grass.

Everything looked so fresh, cold, and clean. There was nothing unusual about it. It was an ordinary garden, an ordinary morning. But she had closed in upon herself; her hands were clenched and her heart was thumping with ever greater anxiety.

"What a cruel, pitiless view!"

She turned away from the window, took a white porcelain cup from the table and, bending down, started attentively studying the gold filigree. Then she suddenly unclenched her fingers. The cup fell noisily to the floor.

Mrs. Roberts stared at the white fragments, lying at her feet, and passed a hand across her brow.

"What is the matter with me?"

She stood and paced around the room. Her anxiety was still growing. She went out into the lobby, then upstairs.

"Where am I going? To see Nina? But she was rude to me yesterday. I can't be the first to speak."

She was about to turn away when she heard a shriek from Nina's room.

"What's going on there?"

She knocked quietly, but no one answered. Then she pushed the half-open door and entered.

The shutters were drawn. The room was almost dark. There was an odor of sal volatile. Nina was lying on the bed. Her dress was unbuttoned. One leg, in a gray silk stocking, hung helplessly to the ground. Her wide-open eyes were directed with fear and surprise upon Mikhail Andreyevich.

"Misha, don't leave me. I'm dying," Nina groaned.

He shrugged his shoulders.

"But the doctor said that there was no danger."

Alexandra Ivanovna bent over her daughter.

"Don't fret, Nina, it's bad for you." She turned to Mikhail Andreyevich. "You…" she began, before suddenly noticing Mrs. Roberts.

Her head shook as if with palsy; her mouth twisted.

"Get out!" she hissed, with hatred. "Get right out of here. Both of you." Mrs. Roberts looked around fearfully.

"What? What are you saying?"

Mikhail Andreyevich took her by the hands. Submissively, she allowed herself to be led away. In the corridor she stopped and burst into tears.

"Why did she chase me away? What did I do?"

He wiped her eyes with his handkerchief, and, bending towards her, said something in a slow, singsong voice.

"What? What's that?"

"I love thee," he repeated in the same tone, carefully mouthing the words. "I love thee…"

Through her tears, she looked confusedly at him; suddenly she guessed that he was teasing her.

"Why are you doing this?"

"I love thee..."

"Why? What does this mean?... Are you serious?"

He put his arms around her.

"Yes, yes, yes. I love thee," he spoke quickly, kissing her lips, her cheeks, her hair. "Now that I'm free, come away with me."

She pulled back from him, fearfully.

"Leave me alone."

But he embraced her more forcefully.

"Let's go, let's go. By car to San Sebastian, and there..."

At last she managed to tear free; she pushed him and ran along the corridor, but he caught her hand again.

"You love me too. Your husband will give you a divorce..."

At the end of the corridor, a maid appeared with a tray. He let go of her hand. She ran away again. The maid watched her go, surprised.

She ran to her room and locked the door.

"What was this?... What did it all mean?"

She threw herself on the bed, sank her head into the pillow. She wept long and bitterly from a sense of hurt, confusion, and self-pity.

Then she rose, washed her face with cold water, and feeling somehow especially weak, light, and miserable, stepping carefully, she went to see her son.

Roy was squatting on his haunches in front of a steamship.

From the window, there was the same familiar, cold, and pitiless view.

She stooped over Roy. Her throat ached with tenderness and love. Here was her life, her joy.

She took the child in her arms, sat in an armchair and, as she rocked him she wept and crooned a Russian rhyme:

The little cat-brother

Had a wicked stepmother

She beat him and scolded...

It grew very quiet. And her worry passed, and her sorrow passed. She sang, pressing the warm child close. It seemed to her that someone else was sitting there and singing. No. It was her mother. Her own mother, holding her in her arms; little Annechka. And she, Annechka, was listening with her tiny face screwed up. How good it felt. How warm. If only it was her mother singing…

The little cat-brother…

But the child suddenly raised his head and looked at her with bright blue sensible eyes.

"Mama, stop, please. I'm bored. Let's go sail the steamship."

1928

KUM[1]

Georgy Peskov (Yelena Deisha)

The night before her wedding, a dream came to Praskovya. The dream was so wild and confused she couldn't make sense of it. That it meant nothing good, she was sure.

This is what Praskovya dreamed: she saw herself stepping over the threshold of her new hut. And there in the hut was her dead mother, seeming to search for something.

"What are you wanting, Ma dear?" said Praskovya to her mother.

"Someone's spilled your dowry," said she, groping on the floor under the benches as she spoke. Praskovya grew frightened. "Leave it, Ma dear," she begged. "Don't look for it, please, there's no need."

And the dead woman answered her: "Just look at this here!" And she held up a pearl: not a fake, but the real thing, a cultured stone. Now, everyone knows what it means to dream of a pearl, and not just any pearl but a cultured one, especially the night before your wedding. Even in her sleep, Praskovya felt afraid at the sight of the jewel. But her mother grew angry. "Take it, you little fool!" she said. "Can't you see? It's yeast. Bake your pies for the wedding feast with it."

And then both the dead woman and the hut vanished. Praskovya found herself walking, all alone, through a snow-covered meadow. It

---

1. In Russian, the word "kum" (and its female equivalent, "kuma") is used by a child's godparents to address one another. By analogy, it can also be used affectionately between close friends. Since there is no direct English equivalent for "kum" ("co-god-parent" might convey the original meaning but not the intimacy), I have left the term untranslated.

was so dark you couldn't see your hand before your face. Well, she thought to herself, I'll look at the gift the gypsy gave me (she fancied then that a gypsy woman – and not her mother – had given her the pearl). As soon as she slipped the gift out of her bosom, everything suddenly grew bright as noontime. She looked down – and a crescent moon was sitting in her hands. "This is my honeymoon," thought Praskovya.

Just then a sleigh drove up out of nowhere. Her betrothed was on it, reining in the horses. "Climb in, Parasha!"[2] he called, tenderly. Praskovya made to step onto the sleigh. The seat was narrow, just like a city *droshky*. Her betrothed, Savel Prokofich, wasn't alone in the sleigh; a stranger was seated right beside him. Praskovya couldn't see his face, but it frightened her. She drew back. And he (not Savel Prokofich, but the other who was with him) cried: "Get in, my dear little *kuma*! There's space for us all. The three of us will surely get there somehow or other. The closer we are, the better friends we'll be."

Once again the scene changed. The sleigh, her betrothed, and the other man were all gone. Praskovya was once more alone in the meadow. But the snow had gone; the meadow was full of standing rye. She could see that her patch of land hadn't been mowed; she must hurry with the reaping. "Alack," she thought, "there's much to be done on my patch."

She started reaping with the crescent-shaped scythe the gypsy had given her. The ears of rye jerked out of her hands, buzzed around her, and pricked her. Blood dripped from Praskovya's face, springing up as red poppies in the meadow. At last Praskovya gave up scything and swatted away the ears of rye, only to see that they were not rye at all, but bees stinging her. "Don't chase us away," they buzzed, "we are gathering honey for your wedding feast." But Praskovya wept: "It's bitter your honey will taste to me, bitter as bile."

---

2. In Russian, most given names have one or more diminutive forms – Natalya becomes Natasha among friends or family, Alexander becomes Sasha. Praskovya is both Parasha and Paranka to her neighbors; Savely is Savel or Savelka (little Savel).

There she woke up, thinking: that was no sort of dream to dream before my wedding day. No good will come of it; it seems Savel and I are not meant to live happily together.

Praskovya hurried off to see Mother White-Eyes, an old woman who lived on the edge of the village, hard by the forest. She was ancient in years, with one eye quite blind and the other missing nothing. She was a capable old woman and could turn her hand to anything: she mixed powders, delivered babies, and read psalms over the departed. She could read your cards and make charms against the evil eye. There was much more the old woman could do, more that was never spoken of. And they called her White-Eyes because both her eyes – the blind and the sighted – were shrouded with a white film.

White-Eyes listened closely to Praskovya's dream: she knew that the visions of young brides are never meaningless. Besides the pearl, which Praskovya herself knew was a bad omen, there were other bad signs (as the old woman read them): first of all, the journey, seemingly a lengthy one. And the journey Savel Prokofich would be making was with a stranger. If the stranger was frightening, that was worse still. But the worst of all was that Praskovya was reaping in her dream. That, said the old woman, was a likely sign of a failed harvest or of an outbreak of sickness, or maybe a murrain among the kine.[3]

As Praskovya was taking her leave, the old woman advised, "Pray to your patron saint as hard as you can. The martyress Paraskeva-Friday will intercede for you against all illnesses, plagues and bad harvests. Make sure that you don't do unclean work on Fridays. God willing, all will be well!"

The old woman's words comforted Praskovya.

The wedding did them all proud. The bride's dress at the altar wouldn't have shamed a priest's daughter. Her gown was made of fine wool, dyed dark red, with a whalebone corset and sleeves that puffed out on top and were trimmed with white lace. It was short in

---

3. Murrain is an antiquated term for an epidemic among cattle or sheep. Kine is a similarly old word designating cattle.

front to show off her new half-boots and had a train behind, as was only proper.

The newlyweds left the church not on a cart, but in a carriage; the driver had been hired from the city. There were two bridesmen: one sat on the driver's bench, with his back to the horses, playing the harmonica, the other on the bridegroom's lap. Both men were decked out in colored blouses and jackets, their curls fluffed up, their caps at a jaunty angle, bellowing out songs.

In a word, it was a fine wedding. And at first, things couldn't have gone better for the young couple. Savel proved to be an easy-going fellow, not one for drink. Praskovya was a good, thrifty housewife. A fine life seemed to beckon them. But things turned out differently. Old Mother White-Eyes's words had been true; a young bride's dreams always mean something. Savel and his young wife hadn't lived together long before war was declared and he was sent off to the German front.

After seeing her husband off on the train, Praskovya fell in a dead faint. But what could be done? Everyone knew that a man had to serve the tsar.

Praskovya was left behind with her mother-in-law; they bore their grief and waited for Savel's letters. Whenever a letter came, her mother-in-law would ask her to try to spell out the words. They were difficult for Praskovya to make sense of. Savel sent his greetings and respects to his dear Mama, and to his beloved spouse, and to all his relatives. The letter would be full of affection and respect, but as for how and what he was doing, there might just be a tiny note: here we sit, he'd write, in the trenches, and we don't know where we'll be sent next.

Praskovya grew wistful. She took to dwelling on the dream she'd had the night before she was wed, which had foretold a parting and a murrain. Perhaps it had threatened even worse things, but Mother White-Eyes had lacked the skill to read the riddles.

The peasants who sold firewood in the city were saying, "Soon the war will be settled. They'll beat the Germans and that Wilhelm of theirs – and then they'll make peace." But half a year went by without peace being made. The Germans were surely sturdy folk. Savel continued to send his respects, and to write nothing about his troubles. After Christmas there wasn't so much as a word from him. How were they to know if he was alive or dead?

Shrovetide came and went, Lent began. Praskovya wrote to Savel: "Your respected mother passed away last week." But even that got no answer. The time came for Praskovya to give birth. Old White-Eyes delivered the baby; they baptized him with his father's name, Savely. When Praskovya recovered, she started begging the peasants in Christ's name to ask in the city for news of her husband. "And how would we find out news of him?" the peasants said to her. Then the village elder took the matter in hand. He asked, "How do you think? Everyone's name must go down on a list, even if they've been killed or taken prisoner." He made inquiries, and told Praskovya later: "Your husband isn't on any of the lists. We have to take it he's alive."

With that, she tried to console herself. Her life had become miserable indeed, especially at harvest time. How was a lone woman to manage on her own – and with an infant as well? Nor did God give them good health.

Then at the beginning of winter, when the roads were firm again, the parish clerk returned from the city and said: "I was talking to a soldier in the town. Now, this soldier was in hospital with Savel Prokofich. He says Savel Prokofich was carried off by typhus."

When Praskovya heard this terrible news, God help us all, she took on so. She wept, howling loud enough to fill the whole hut, speaking to Savel as if he were still living with her, before she toppled to the ground, twisting in convulsions. She was terrible to look upon. Old White-Eyes nursed her, staying in Savel's hut until the second cock-crow, making the widow drink herbal tinctures, sprinkling her with blessed water. Long after midnight Praskovya, lulled by all the potions and spells, fell asleep. Once she was asleep, Old White-Eyes gave the child a dummy to suck, and went to her own home. Even an old person needs rest sometimes.

Praskovya woke soon enough. Savelka had dropped his dummy and started wailing. She rose, took the child in her arms and gave him the breast. She herself was half-asleep; her mind was clouded, she barely remembered what had happened the day before. Suddenly someone knocked on the door. Praskovya opened it – and froze on the spot. There in the yard – and morning hadn't even broken yet – stood a soldier in a tall astrakhan hat and a worn-out greatcoat, ragged strips of cloth wound about his neck. He was shivering all over. As soon as Praskovya saw the soldier, her heart began to beat again. Her memory returned to her, and she recalled yesterday's events.

The soldier stood on the threshold. He was hideously ugly; his face was fearsome, even. He was all white, as if sprinkled with flour, but his nose was red and narrow. His face, God forgive us, was just like the masks that children wear at Shrovetide. His eyes were half-slitted, blinking constantly.

"Greetings to you, *kuma*," he said. "Don't you know me?"

Praskovya stared at him.

"I never set eyes on you in my life, I'm sure."

"It's the truth you're saying, my dear little *kuma*," answered the soldier, "we meet now for the first time. But there's no harm in that, for I come to you not with evil tidings, but with good news."

"There's no good news you can bring me now," said Praskovya.

"Only listen before you judge if my news is good or not."

"It has nothing to do with me. Go back where you came from."

"Don't chase me away, *kuma*. I'll say one word, and you'll beg me to stay." Then he whispered low: "Prokofich sends his respects."

"What?" screeched Praskovya.

"Your husband sends you greetings, I said."

Praskovya's heart shuddered. She stared at the soldier's ugly face, not knowing whether to believe his words. She dearly wanted to trust them.

"Can he really be living?" she whispered.

"And in good health."

Praskovya's hands started to tremble.

"Come into the hut."

He came in. He didn't pray to the icons, nor raise his hat from his head. But Praskovya saw none of this. "Tell me about him, don't make me suffer!" she urged her guest. "Where is he, how is he keeping?"

"In German captivity," answered the guest. "We had hard times together there, working on empty stomachs, suffering their beatings. There we got to know each other, there we became each other's *kum* – the best of friends."

Here the visitor began to tell her about Savel in such a lively way – describing all his habits and his little ways – that no one could doubt they must have lived together a long time. From the tales he told, Praskovya began to trust him. She grew friendly toward him, and she herself began calling the strange soldier "*kum*."

"Well then," said the visitor, "my dear little *kuma*, won't you show me Savel's heir?"

Praskovya lifted the child out of the cradle. The soldier took Savelka in his arms and grinned at him, showing his swollen gums. They looked as if someone had pulled out half his teeth; they were terribly sparse, and as sharp and crooked as awls. Once again he struck Praskovya as fearsome. She was afraid he might put the evil eye on her. Who knew what was going on in his head? Perhaps he hadn't been Savel's best friend at all, but some ill-wisher. The infant also seemed to sense something awry; he began crying. Praskovya hurriedly laid her son back in the cradle.

"How come they let you out of prison?" she began questioning the soldier again.

"Is there anyone else in the hut?" asked her visitor, stealing a sidelong glance at the stove.

"Who else would there be?" Praskovya replied.

"Then listen, *kuma*. I'll tell you, as long as you don't pass on a single word of mine."

"I swear on the Cross, *kum*, I'll keep quiet."

Once again the soldier swept a cautious gaze around the hut.

"Savel and I escaped from prison together," he said.

"Really? Holy Mother of God! Then where can he be?"

The visitor fiddled with the rag wrapped around his neck.

"He'll be here soon, within seven days at the most. But keep quiet until he comes, so that empty talk doesn't go round the village. Keep it to yourself, not a word to others. Mind that you don't get Savel into trouble."

"What are you saying, *kum*? Have no doubts: no one will hear of it from me. But why is he hiding like this?"

The soldier sniggered, nastily.

"And how could he do other than hide," he said, "after what he got up to?"

Praskovya didn't have a notion what the *kum* meant. Perhaps he had in mind Savel's escape from the prison camp?

"There's no Germans here he'd need to hide from!" she said.

"You're not the sharpest, are you, *kuma*? Forgive me for speaking harshly, but it's true what they say about women being long of hair and short of wit. Listen to me: if word gets out about this matter, if it reaches the officers, your husband will be walking the long road to prison in Siberia. Do you understand that?"

Praskovya understood very little, but she was too ashamed to ask more. She sensed something amiss behind the *kum*'s words.

"And why didn't the two of you come here together?"

Praskovya's questions clearly weren't to the *kum*'s liking. He answered reluctantly: "We travelled together over the German territory, but once we were on Russian soil, we said our goodbyes: he went his way, and I went mine."

"Why was that, since you were going the same road?"

The soldier lost his temper. "'Why, why!' You, *kuma*, are a tiresome nag. One might be talking to you until tomorrow."

"Forgive my foolish ways, *kum*. Why, I haven't even offered you a bite to eat or a drink," Praskovya exclaimed. She made to offer the porridge that Mother White-Eyes had left on the stove.

"Thank you, *kuma*," said the visitor, in a softer tone. "I'm grateful, but I've had my fill. On my way to you, I turned off the road, I'll admit, at the alehouse by the graveyard, and I stuffed my belly."

"What ale-house by the graveyard?" Praskovya thought. "There's no alehouse there." But she kept her puzzlement to herself; she didn't dare question her guest.

"Well, farewell, *kuma*! I've stayed on with you to the third cockcrow."

"Where are you hurrying to, my dear? I'm so glad of your coming! I'm right grateful for the news you brought… Indeed I can't be easy in my mind; how can I show you my gratitude?"

"It's nothing, *kuma*. What would I be taking from you? There's just one thing you could do, if it's not too troublesome. Say this to your husband: your *kum*, tell him, asks for that little debt to be paid back. He'll know what you mean."

"Very well, *kum*, I'll tell him surely."

"And one more thing, if you've any kindness for me, do me one little favor more, *kuma*."

"Ask what you will, *kum*. I'm glad to do whatever I can."

"The task isn't hard: think of me at your prayers, my dear, every morning and evening. When you pray for the health of your father and mother, then pray for me too."

Praskovya wanted to tell him that she didn't pray for her parents' health, but for their rest, as both of them had passed away long ago. But she held her tongue.

"I'll do it, my benefactor, I will," she said. "I'll do it without fail, with all my heart. And what is your Christian name?"

"They christened me Levonty. Well then!" With that, he said, "I beg your pardon and thank you for your affectionate welcome."

As Praskovya saw him over the threshold, she added:

"I'll pray for you, my benefactor, until they lay me in my grave. And for your dear wife also, if you'll allow, and your little children, if God has blessed you with them."

"I thank you, *kuma*. I've neither wife nor children. I'm a lonely bachelor. No one to make the sign of the cross over me in the whole world. If you'll say a prayer for this sinner's soul, I thank you. So there we are, *kuma*… And tell your husband, if you will, not to forget: tell him to remember that little debt. He'll know."

With those words he walked away. Praskovya watched him go, thinking: "A strange fellow: we must have sat together an hour or more, and it's still just as dark outside as it was, and not a sign of the sun." Deep in thought, she went back into the hut, lay down again on her narrow bed, and dozed off.

In the morning, Old Mother White-Eyes came. She found the inconsolable widow of the day before primping in front of the mirror.

"It's plain to see, she's lost her reason," the old woman thought. "Praskovya!" she called, "what are you doing that for?"

"As you see, I'm looking myself over," said Praskovya. "When Prokofich comes back later, he won't know me. 'You're skin and bones,' he'll say, 'you've lost your looks.'"

"What's happened to you, you poor troubled soul? Have you gone mad?" the old woman studied the widow with her white eyes.

Then Praskovya remembered the visitor had warned her not to say a word about Savel's return to anyone, for fear of misfortune. She began pleading, begging the old woman to keep quiet. She dared not tell her about the *kum's* visit. Instead she pretended to have dreamed that Savel would certainly return very soon. And she thought to herself, "Who knows? Perhaps I really did see it all in a vision, if not a dream. Only it was all so terribly clear… I can see him now, with that cloth wrapped around his neck, or whatever kind of rag it was…" And as Praskovya recalled that rag wrapped so tightly around his neck, her heart ached again with grief.

Praskovya waited all day. And all of the next day. And all of the third. The week wore to an end. No Savel came back from German captivity. Praskovya was seized by doubt: could the stranger have lied to her? Was he really a friend of Savel's, as he'd claimed? The *kum's* words came back to her, dark and fearsome. And as soon as ever she tried to pray for the soul of the humble sinner Levonty, somehow the prayer died on her lips. It was as if a stone lay on her heart, growing heavier as the days passed.

And then, a week later to the day, Savel came back. His wife – and the neighbors too – gasped at the sight of him. He looked like a ghost returned from the other world: pale, puffy, red-eyed. No one would have known him as the old Savel, before the Germans captured him. He was Savel, but not Savel. He had been a friendly fellow, especially with Praskovya. He had had a fine turn of speech. Now he uttered each word reluctantly, as if struggling to speak. Then he'd fall silent again. He never wanted to describe the battles, or the prison camp, or his wanderings afterwards: I'm sick of it, he would say. He wouldn't take Savelka in his arms. Praskovya took offence; it was as if he thought the child wasn't his. She tried to tell him about the visitor: "Your *kum* came and brought me tidings of you."

Savel yelled at her, "What *kum* are you talking about? I don't know what you mean! Why are you telling lies about things you don't understand? I have no *kum*!"

Praskovya bit her tongue. She could see something wasn't right here. She remembered how the *kum* had scared her with the long road to Siberia.

"Well," Savel asked her after a pause, "have you been gabbling to anyone in the village about this?"

"Not to anyone," Praskovya answered, "I didn't speak a word,"

"That's as it should be. And in future mind you don't let anything slip. And now you forget about this *kum* of yours, if you can."

Praskovya wanted to mention the "little debt," but she was afraid.

Savel went to the big town. He reported at the local military office, without a thought of hiding himself. He came home with a white ticket of discharge. So the *kum*'s menaces had been empty.

Wife and husband lived as they had before, but not quite. Savel's brows frowned ever more darkly. Praskovya followed her husband with her eyes. She saw that he had acquired heathen manners; he never put a foot inside the church, never crossed himself. When Praskovya didn't serve meat at dinner, he turned up his nose.

"What's the matter," said Praskovya, "won't you taste some?"

"There's no flavor to it. You might have added some fat for taste."

"Listen to yourself! It's Friday."

"What difference does that make?"

"I see that in captivity with the heathens you forgot your faith in Christ?"

"And maybe I did forget," he said. "We have one faith, they have another. Who knows which of us is right? And meanwhile, whichever faith you follow, we're all cutthroats at heart."

"Come now," Praskovya replied, "that's what men do in wartime. Can you really be held accountable?"

Savel sneered.

"Indeed you can," he said, "indeed you can."

"It's one matter to kill someone in war," said Praskovya, "another to commit murder on the high road."

The look Savel fixed on her was terrible. He clenched his fist around the bread knife he had been using a moment before.

"What road," he said, "are you talking about?"

He spoke quietly, spacing his words. His face was as pale as a pocket-handkerchief. Praskovya turned white as death too.

"I… Prokofich, I was talking about robbers," she said.

"You're lying!" Savel shouted suddenly. "I can see by your eyes that you're lying! Go on – tell me what tales he spun about me."

"Who are you talking about, my dear one? I don't understand a thing…"

"Oh don't you?" Savel flung the knife away. "I suppose you saw it all in a dream." Muttering, he left the table. He spent a long time rooting around by the front door, searching for something. Praskovya sat there, more dead than alive, until Savel came back into the room.

"Listen, wife," he said. "Let this be the last time we speak of this matter. If you know something about it, say nothing to remind me. Don't drive me to sin."

Praskovya understood nothing of her husband's words. She guessed one thing only, and it made her sick to her stomach. She guessed there was no longer any need to pray for the health of the humble sinner Levonty.

That winter was a terrible one. Savel carried on like a madman, neither eating nor sleeping, and knowing no peace. Praskovya was tormented by evil dreams. Sometimes she would hear wolves howling, and in her dream she would wonder whether the door was firmly locked. She would glance towards the door, and Savel's *kum* would be standing there. Or she would dream she was milking the cow, and again she would look up and see the *kum*, asking for a sup of milk. He would raise the pail and drink. And instead of milk, the pail would brim with blood.

Praskovya would wake in terror to see that Savel had got down from the stove and was pacing back and forth in the hut. Then he'd go stand in the cold entryway, talking to himself out there. Praskovya's thoughts wandered as she lay sleepless on the stove. Their household had gone to pieces: the roof had rotted through, snow was leaking into the hut. They had to sell the cow before the summer was even over; they had to buy grain as early as Christmas, and grain was expensive. Savel was no good as a worker now; his legs pained him, his bones ached; he was no longer the man he had been. And would that these had been their only troubles!

As fate would have it, that winter was long and brutal. There seemed to be no end to it. The snow fell so heavily they couldn't leave the hut, and blizzards howled constantly. Once Praskovya had to go to the priest to borrow a saw; theirs had grown too blunt. It was already getting on for night. Her way lay past the churchyard. Between the drifts of snow the gray crosses seemed to stretch out their arms in the dark, as if longing to seize her. Praskovya was terrified. The wind tore her flannel scarf from her head, and the snow blinded her eyes. Just as she was about to turn towards the priest's house, from behind the church someone called out to her in a pitiful voice: "*Kuuu-mmaa, kuuuu-mmmmaaa....*"

Praskovya shrieked in a voice that wasn't her own, and rushed home without looking back. "I found no one in at the Father's," she told her husband.

She said nothing about how the *kum* had alarmed her.

That same night Savel was taken ill. He was burning hot and freezing cold by turns. "I must have caught a chill on my chest last night, sawing wood," he said. Praskovya knew straight away that his time had come. Savel never said a word before he died about his sin. Nor did Praskovya dare to mention it. She wanted to call the priest, but Savel said, "No need for that!" And so he died, without repenting. Until the last he was raking his breast with his hand, seeking something. Praskovya thought he was in pain. But when she started to dress the dead man in a clean shirt, she found a rag tightly bound against his breast. Inside it was a wad of paper money; strange stuff, a kind she'd never seen. Praskovya thought about it for a long time, and then she hid it as deep as she could in a chest.

Sorrows follow close as sisters, as they say. An illness began running through the children. A child would lay down to sleep in the evening quite healthy, and wake up in the night with a cry, grabbing his neck as if someone were strangling him. In his throat his breath creaked and gurgled. After suffering a fever through the night, he'd be laid out the next morning. Praskovya's son was one of the first to sicken. She took on like a madwoman, weeping and cursing, making the neighbors marvel at her: "We never knew Paranka had any secrets, but now she keeps calling on some *kum* of hers: Come, I beg you, *kum*, says she, I pray you in the name of Christ, take your damned money, lift your curse!"

The little boy lasted less than a day before dying. Praskovya also seemed less than alive. She could neither pray nor bewail her loss. She looked with dry eyes on Savelka's waxy face, and laughed bitterly. When they were digging Savelka's grave in the frozen ground, Praskovya turned with a wave of her hand and went straight home, saying calmly, almost gladly, "Let him lie! He's warm now."

From that day, Praskovya grew talkative. Before long, she revealed it all. Old Mother White-Eyes, who kept her company, learned about Savel's sin, and the *kum*'s money. She even learned that the *kum* came to Praskovya every night, tempting her to unclean acts. The old woman fixed her white eyes – one blind, one sighted – on Praskovya and listened for a long time. Then she set off through the village to warn the other women to sprinkle all the corners and walls of their huts, their doors and the path around the village with a potion distilled from garlic. They should give their children the same thing to drink. And if their husbands asked them why they were doing it, they were to say "For tapeworms," so no questions would be asked.

And this was how they made the potion: they took a head of garlic, split it into cloves, shredded these into tiny pieces with a knife, mixed it with boiling water and left it to distil. That way the mixture came out whitish and smelled strongly.

Since it was clear that the German money was at the bottom of all her misfortunes, the old woman told Praskovya to burn it, and never even once to pray for Levonty's soul: "If you do that," she said, "you'll call him back to you. Whatever sin your husband may have committed," she said, "God will settle it, and it's not for us to meddle in this business."

1929

THE MOTHER

Nadezhda Teffi

Blessed are the pains of separation, of humiliation, of insult, and blessed is the bitter ecstasy of self-denial. Blessed is love of any kind. And blessed, a thousand times over, is a mother's love: the most self-sacrificing, the most scorned, the only love that bears out the apostle's words that she "seeketh not for herself."

The love between lovers is splendid and festive. Its raiment is silk and purple. It sings and dances. It beautifies itself in order to seize, to conquer, and to keep what it has seized.

A mother's love yields up its silk and purple raiment.

On dreary weekdays, in rags and tatters, this love climbs steep slopes, led by a silent shade with a fiery halo on its head, its breast pierced by seven swords and covered by a meagre cloak.[1]

And now I want to tell you of one such blessed love, a vast, powerful, glorious love, ringing out in our dull world like a divine and stellar symphony never before heard by human ears: the story of Madame Beauvais' love for her little boy, Paul.

---

1. Teffi's imagery in this passage draws on both written and visual religious tradition. The first allusion is to a passage in St. Paul's First Letter to the Corinthians (13:5). St. Paul writes that charity "seeketh not her own, is not easily provoked, thinketh no evil"; while not explicitly maternal, this clearly describes selfless love. Teffi's reference to "silk and purple raiment" is from the Old Testament, namely Proverbs (31:22), where a virtuous woman is described as one who "maketh herself coverings of tapestry; her clothing is silk and purple." Finally, the image of the shade climbing the hill is derived from a well-known Orthodox Christian icon showing the Virgin Mary with her bosom pierced by seven swords, each sword symbolizing one of the sorrows of her life.

In the imagination of any lover – surely you've noticed? – the age of their loved one has nothing to do with their physical age. They live eternally at one particular moment in time, imprinted on the lover's heart. I remember how one affectionate wife, meeting her husband in a restaurant, asked the doorman:

"Has a dark, slender man with a black moustache come in just now?"

"No," replied the doorman. "There's only a rather fat old man who just arrived – he's bald and clean-shaven. He's sitting over there."

She turned, and recognized her husband.

For Charlotte Beauvais, her Paul would always remain a boy of two: chubby, captious, and defenseless. He was "her little boy Paul." When she looked at the thickset, sturdy young man with his square face and short neck, she saw a plump little face with dimples. She saw herself lathering his curly head with soap, as he stood, short and stumpy, in the basin. He didn't cry: he just grunted, stretched out his stubby little arm, and pinched her breast with all his strength, hurting her. His tiny fingers with their tiny narrow nails, like wedges of glass, sank in as hard as they could, pressing down on and tearing the skin, and she laughed from tenderness and sympathy because this pitiful little boy was trying to protect himself yet could not defeat her, however much he wanted, and all because she was bathing him…

"Paul! My little boy!"

Madame Beauvais had spent her youth in Russia. She had been a governess; she married a French bank clerk. Then she buried her husband and, after the revolution, she brought her Paul, already a youth of seventeen, to Paris.

Paul did not wish to continue his education. He decided to take up business. He started selling Russian liqueurs and smoked fish in restaurants. Madame Beauvais knitted scarves and cardigans. They lived, always hungry and cold, in one of the *faubourgs* of Paris.[2] Two

---

2. The Russian word "predmestye," which Teffi uses, is often translated as *faubourg*, so the meaning here is "near suburb," just outside the city, rather than the more distant modern *banlieu*.

friends often visited Paul – a Frenchman and a Russian. They ate up whatever food there was in the house, and sometimes they stayed the night too. They never said a word to Madame Beauvais, as if they did not even notice her presence. They smoked and played cards. The word "turkey" often recurred in their exchanges:

"Paul, have the turkey do it!"

"You've really let that turkey get out of hand!"

"Can you really not pluck just two little feathers off the turkey for the metro?"

"That turkey's no good. It's filled its belly with chestnuts, and it doesn't care about anyone else."

She soon understood that "turkey" was their nickname for her, but she did not dare to take offence. She feared the boys; she feared they would take Paul away from her home. He was constantly threatening to leave; he was demanding, and rude, and discontented with everything.

"Slurp your own coffee; I'm not going to drink that swill."

"Paulie, my sweet. Didn't I give you all the last of the sugar? Look – I drink mine with no sugar at all."

"That's a dumb argument. It doesn't make my coffee any sweeter."

A time came when the boys had run through all their money and moved right in with Paul. They lounged around, smoking and, for want of anything better to do, making fun of the "turkey," no longer holding back.

And then and there Madame Beauvais was inspired: determinedly and at length, she rummaged through her old packing box and her bags and bundles until she found an address book. And then she set off. Thus began a new era in her life.

She searched out other Russian emigrants, people she had known in the past, and cadged a few francs from each of them. On the first day she got a whole hundred francs right away and, breathless from shame and pride, she brought the money to Paul. His joyfully shining eyes were, for her, an intoxicating reward. He even hugged her.

"Dear old turkey, what a clever girl you are!"

She smiled, squeezing her lips together so as not to shout or whimper from the extremity of her happiness.

From that day, it was as if she had joined the boys' gang. Her entire bearing even became sprightlier.

"The turkey's going to get us twenty francs."

"The turkey's a star."

She felt like their older comrade, someone to reckon with, someone to rely on. Their regard rewarded her for the long years of humiliation. And she worked conscientiously. She went into the city early. She would drink a cup of coffee in a *bistro*, standing up, often without any bread (that was for her lunch), then work her way around her client list. She borrowed from the most unlikely people: a baker's wife to whom she already owed something, an old Russian nanny, a poor schoolteacher, a French general, a seamstress who had once made over her dress in her first days in Paris, a Russian writer, a Polish hairdresser. If they didn't have twenty francs, she would take ten; if they didn't have ten, two would do. It was all the same to her. She was no longer embarrassed by an unfriendly reception. She no longer even noticed it. She would sit down and, without any explanations, begin in a dull, grating voice:

"My boy's been promised a place. He just has to wait nine days, at the most. But we need to eat something for those nine days. Even if you allow just eight francs a day, well, that makes…"

"In four days' time my boy is supposed to start a new job. And what's he got to wear? His coat's pawned for thirty francs, and then there's the interest on it…"

Or:

"My boy's been given a splendid position. We just have to hold out until his first paycheck, and the concierge won't wait for the rent…"

Soon everyone knew her gray silhouette even from far away, that hat with a pheasant feather, down which rain always ran as if through a gutter onto her right shoulder, her thin wiry legs on unevenly worn-down heels. And if she did not succeed in catching someone, she hid in the foyer and waited until her victim returned.

Naturally modest and honest, she had no awareness of shame or of her own lies. She was working for her "little boy" – that captious, defenseless little thing. He had grown up, but in essence he was still the same child.

"My little boy. Look what your faithful turkey's brought you. Seventeen francs – are you happy?"

But her "work" became more and more difficult. Her victims began ever more readily and sharply refusing her; they cold-bloodedly slammed the door in her face. Her earnings fell to five or six francs a day. And right away, her standing in the household, which she had won with such effort, changed drastically. The young men left. Paul stopped talking to her. Then he started disappearing for two or three days at a time. From throwaway remarks, she gathered that he was working in some sort of garage... Then one time he turned up in a nice suit, with pomaded hair, and said that he was marrying Ernestine, the garage owner's daughter. But there was no reason for her to meet the new relatives.

"He's ashamed of me, the poor boy!" thought Madame Beauvais, and her heart filled with sorrow and tenderness. "Why, you've little enough reason to be proud of me, Paulie, my little boy..."

Long, dead days went by in her quiet room... It was so quiet that she herself began to tiptoe; the tap of her feet would have been terrifying, like the sound of steps in a vault, in the house of the dead.

She received a printed card informing her of the wedding between Paul Beauvais and Mademoiselle Ernestine Cloux.

Ernestine... What a strange, cross name. That wicked *r*. She must be dark, with a long nose. And ugly. And even if she was beautiful, so much the worse; her little boy would be stolen even further away. As things were, he hadn't even come to see his mother before the wedding. Of course, it must be the girl who wouldn't let him go, who didn't want his own mother to give him her blessing. Ernestine... Ernestine...

She took to chatting with Ernestine; she forgave her for everything, because the boy loved her, and she hated her for the same reason. She suffered particularly from the thought that he was almost certainly chatting with *her*…

"But after all, married happiness rarely lasts very long. The boy will be disillusioned; he'll come to see his faithful old turkey to rest his soul. He'll come, even just for a minute or two."

And she daydreamed like a fifteen-year-old girl, picturing some unexpected disaster:

"Ernestine has drowned, or burnt to death, but my little boy isn't grieving, because he'd fallen out of love with her already. Ernestine has accidentally poisoned herself – accidentally…"

She shivered – startled by her ball of yarn tumbling off her knee.

These dead days were killing her. She aged visibly, let herself go, became untidy, forgot to comb her hair. She left home once a week in order to deliver what she'd knitted and to buy bread, cheese, eggs. She worked poorly, dropped stitches, left holes, turned in knitting that was straggly and grubby. That was how she lived through her dead days.

And then one morning there was a firm, insistent knock at the door.

She opened it reluctantly.

"My little boy!"

The whole room seemed to dance around her, singing, ringing like a bell. The blinds on the windows rattled – as if they were breathing! – the taps whistled, the lid of the cafetière clattered, the floorboards squeaked, the old wardrobe crepitated, the wicker armchair creaked, straightening its seat and armrests: everything came back to life!

"Sit down, my little one, my dear little boy. You came after all!"

Uncomfortable and uncomprehending, he watched her weep.

"How old and dirty you look."

His voice! He was speaking! What a wonderful thing life was after all!

Little Paulie didn't stay for long. He didn't tell her anything definite, but she knew in her heart that he did not love Ernestine.

She also found out that the owner of the garage was old and sick, and that his business would be left to Paul. But that wasn't important. For her, the important thing was that her little boy did not love Ernestine.

More days passed – living and dead.

Sometimes she felt with absolute clarity that the boy would visit that day. And then she did up her hair and dressed up nicely.

Perhaps he had come to love Ernestine? Let him. She herself was ready to make him believe that Ernestine was sweet and good. All that mattered was his happiness. For it was all the same to her whether a good or a wicked woman had emptied out her life. Whether she died by the sword or by a dirty safety-pin. It was the same death. It was the same emptiness…

The living and dead days went on for a long time. Then they ended abruptly: Paul arrived. He looked bloated, pale, disturbed.

"They've tricked me," he said. "Ernestine's pregnant, and the old man's leaving everything to the kid. And I'll spend my whole life working for them. Mother! Help me. Think of something."

Ernestine was pregnant. There was a horror which she, Madame Beauvais, had never even dared to think about. A child! You can love a child so much… There it was, there it was indeed, the most terrifying thing. A child would take Paul away from her forever. But she had to answer him. He looked angry and plaintive and he was waiting.

"What do you want, my little boy? Perhaps all will be well and you will love your own child."

Afterwards she often dreamt of the terrifying fury that had rippled swiftly across his trembling face.

A few days later a letter from him arrived, written in French:

"My dear *maman*! My wife and I are going to Chartres tomorrow. We will call for you. I kiss you. Paul."

A strange letter. Almost as if he'd written it to order.

They arrived that evening.

"We'll spend the night with you, and drive on in the morning. You'll come with us."

Ernestine was tall, flat-chested, gray, very ugly. Her boy's wife... Madame Beauvais wanted to embrace her and weep. Her boy's wife... She remembered that transient warmth in her bosom for a long time afterwards. All the rest of what happened, as unusual, unlikely, monstrous and simple as it was, lay like a shifting cloud at the very base of her mind.

She remembered that they stayed the night, and that Ernestine wept in her sleep. They left early in the morning. Paul was at the wheel, she and Ernestine sat together. Ernestine was on the right.

Then, in a wood, Paul suddenly stopped the car and got out. His face was frightened and stubborn, painfully strained. He went around to the right-hand side. She wanted to ask what had happened, but she didn't dare – his face was terrible, so terrible that the sound of the gunshot didn't even startle Madame Beauvais. She had read that gunshot on his face. Then he jumped swiftly into his seat and started the car, while Ernestine drooped her head and sank onto Madame Beauvais' shoulder. She would remember, and feel, for many, many days to come the weight of that body and the scent of Ernestine's woolen scarf.

When the houses of the next town came into view, Paul turned to her and yelled,

"She was shot by robbers, but we didn't see them! Got it?"

And he revved the car.

When she was summoned for questioning as a witness and she saw the prisoner's rough, fat face set on a short neck, collarless, she did not immediately recognize her son.

"That's a criminal," she thought, with revulsion.

The idiotic invention about robbers had been knocked down straightaway. Paul was being tried as a murderer.

"But he really, really loved his wife," Madame Beauvais repeated stupidly.

"I'm innocent," said Paul, plaintively.

At the sound of that voice she turned her head and met his eyes. His eyes were asking her:

"Well, what are you going to do?"

They were begging:

"Help me! Think of something!"

She watched calmly and thought, with revulsion,

"A criminal."

And suddenly his lips trembled, his brow twitched, and barely noticeable dimples spread over his cheeks… Her boy! Her little boy, it was him… It was him!

And suddenly, not understanding herself or knowing what she was doing, she flung herself on her knees and cried in a voice that came from her whole body:

"Forgive me, my little boy, forgive me!"

And he answered loudly:

"Mama, you poor dear."

And he added quietly:

"I forgive you."

She didn't even hear that monstrous "I forgive you." "Mama, you poor dear" had deafened her soul like the crash of a cymbal; she lost consciousness.[3]

When they took her from the prison to the court, many days later, an expanded police guard protected her from the "people's outrage against the witch who killed her daughter-in-law out of jealousy for her son."

She looked dreadful. Her dry face, sharp as a sabre-blade, peeped from under a hat with a broken pheasant feather that had seen better days. Covered in red patches from nervous eczema, her face appeared to be burning. Her gray lips smiled, and her quivering eyes, in their dark sockets, gleamed with pearly light.

---

3. The image of the cymbal is taken from St. Paul's First Letter to the Corinthians, 13:1.

The crowd howled:

"She's laughing, the monster!"

"Send her to the guillotine!"

"Death to the old camel!"

"Death to the old camel," her lips repeated, smiling beatifically.

Perhaps she did not fully understand the words she repeated. More than likely, she did not. Light and noise had filled her world. The vast symphony of her life, divine and cruel, was finally resolved in a single chord, calm and blissful.

"So it had to be. Only this way – with wisdom and beauty. Here he comes, the Father, slaking the thirst of the crucified."

Blessed is the love.

1929

AN ADVENTURER

Gaito Gazdanov

Anna Sergeyevna had left the ball, once again, like two days before, without waiting for the end of the third or fourth dance; and yet again, she could not explain her compulsion to depart so early. In truth, she felt, there was no particular reason. She loved dancing and dreaded solitude just as much as ever; and, just as ever, not one even moderately important event in Petersburg life of that time could take place without her indirect involvement. But lately, although Anna Sergeyevna hadn't exactly lost interest, it had all become just another of those long-familiar habits; essential, but not enough in themselves to entirely occupy her extensive leisure or to satisfy her constant yet formless expectation of a certain thing that might or might not take place. When and how it might happen, Anna Sergeyevna could not imagine. A long, long time ago, she had thought that all would be revealed to her when she married; then she decided that marriage had betrayed her expectations and that her real passion was for art; then she supposed that Lieutenant Sokolov might replace both her husband and her dilettantish studies in literature and music; but even Lieutenant Sokolov proved, on closer acquaintance, to be dull. A month ago, her second fortunate admirer, her husband's new secretary, had gone abroad with his employer; and at first Anna Sergeyevna had thought that she would struggle to cope without his almost constant presence, his jokes, his verses and his French compliments, or without experiencing his inexplicable magnetism, which she was quite unable to resist; and

yet within a week she had stopped thinking about him. She did not spend too long brooding over these things, not wishing to spoil her own humor; but this unjustified sense of expectation was with her always, no less unpleasant than the fraying hem of a dress or powder flaking off her skin.

She was driven slowly through the town, which was silent and chilly; every now and then one heard the frozen snow splitting or echoing underfoot. The coachman sat up on his box as unmoving as a boulder; the horse went almost at a walk; there was hardly any wind, the streets were white and deserted. And then, passing the Humpback Bridge, beyond which a long, fantastical row of stone houses stood out in relief against the snow and the low sky, Anna Sergeyevna saw a man seated on a curbstone, the collar of his fur coat raised. He sat there unmoving, his head sunk deeply into his collar, without looking ahead; and at first sight it even occurred to her that the man had fallen asleep, before she suddenly realized that he was not sleeping. But she could not have explained how she knew that: nothing had changed in the seated man's pose. Anna Sergeyevna suddenly conceived a strange wish to look more closely at this man. She ordered the coachman to halt, stepped out of her sleigh, and walked over to the curb. As she came closer, her steps grew hesitant; at that moment she thought the man was staring directly at her feet. Nonetheless, she walked right up to him – and asked, in a voice changed by long silence, "What are you doing here?"

He raised his head, and Anna Sergeyevna opened her eyes wide; she had never yet seen a face like this. The man was unusually handsome, with startlingly symmetrical features in a faultlessly oval face. Yet it was not this that struck Anna Sergeyevna, but rather, the man's expression. An indefinably abnormal, almost insane quality somehow just failed to spoil that classical face.

He made no reply to Anna Sergeyevna's question, merely smiling and shrugging slightly.

"You don't wish to answer?" said Anna Sergeyevna, with sudden ire. Then he gave her a surprised look. "Perhaps he's a foreigner," thought Anna Sergeyevna, and she said uncertainly:

"Do you understand Russian?"

"No," came the clear answer in a manly tenor.

"What language do you speak?" Anna Sergeyevna asked in French. How strange, she told herself; he speaks no Russian, sits here alone at night – who can he be? Some *aventurier*?

"I would be happy if you wish to speak in French," he replied. He spoke rapid and accurate French, enunciating the words over-carefully and endowing them with that almost untraceable metallic intonation that always distinguishes the speech of a foreigner, even one who may know the language better than a native, from that of a Frenchman. Anna Sergeyevna, however, paid no attention to this.

"Whatever are you doing here?" she repeated.

"I am sitting and watching and occasionally I close my eyes, so as to better remember what I see. Do you know," he said, suddenly raising his voice, "have you ever thought, glancing around at night in Petersburg, have you ever thought that the end of the world, when it comes, will be very much like this? I don't think that a catastrophe or an earthquake or a flood will come to pass; no, our descendants will simply freeze, gazing just like this at the beautiful buildings, buried in the whiteness and the sounds of the snow, just as you and I are looking at them now. Tomorrow I will leave Petersburg," he remarked, without any connection to what he had just said.

Anna Sergeyevna did not answer the foreigner at once; his voice, and the words he was speaking, suddenly seemed to her of a piece with this night-time street in Petersburg, its hardened snow and dark buildings, the coachman frozen on his box and the unmoving horse, like a black statue, and with the whole of this strange and random evening. She was silent, suddenly contemplative, exactly as if the normal course of her thoughts and sensations had halted unexpectedly. Then she glanced at her companion; he was standing, slightly hunched, his hands thrust into his pockets, gazing before him with straining eyes which appeared to be trying to draw in everything that surrounded them. An odd vertical wrinkle bisected his forehead, which was gleaming in the frost.

"And what is it your intention to do now?" asked Anna Sergeyevna. He coughed a little, laughed, and answered with a smile,

"I will come to visit you, if you have no objection. Don't be angry with me," he said, noticing Anna Sergeyevna's frown. "If you don't want me to come, I will wish you all the best and I will wait here for morning, without you."

An adventurer, Anna Sergeyevna thought once again. All the same… all the same, one could invite him to visit.

"Perfect," she said. "I invite you to my house. Now is hardly the time for visiting, but after all you are leaving tomorrow, and we won't see each other again."

"Never," the adventurer said firmly.

"Never? Are you quite sure of that?"

"I know it. But, perhaps, you might prefer to discuss this at your home. I am very cold," he said, his tone unexpectedly almost childish.

So they drove off. Houses swept swiftly past them; they passed the massive building of the Engineers' Castle, off to one side the heavy outlines of the Winter Palace sketched themselves in the frosty air and disappeared, a wide ribbon of ice under the bridge slipped by, and at last the coachman stopped the frothing horse in front of one of the low houses on Sergiyev Street.

"Here we are," said Anna Sergeyevna.

He climbed down from the sleigh and helped her to alight; the heavy door was opened immediately, and they found themselves in the entryway, where a twelve-year-old servant-boy was sleeping; his open mouth and pale childish face involuntarily expressed genuine bewilderment.

"Vasya," said Anna Sergeyevna softly, smiling. "Vasya," she repeated, as the startled boy bolted up from the narrow couch where he had lain, "why are you so startled, my dear? What were you dreaming about? Well?"

"I'm very sorry, marm," the boy said in an unexpectedly firm tone, "I dozed off."

"Well, go on then, my dear," said Anna Sergeyevna tenderly. "Just take the gentleman's coat first."

"You'll forgive me," she spoke again in French, turning to the adventurer, "I will return in a moment. Wouldn't you like to go into the sitting room?"

"*Excusez*," whispered the boy approvingly. And then, when he took the gentleman's coat, he said aloud, in an enquiring tone, "*Excusez?*"

"Yes, indeed," said the adventurer, smiling and patting the boy on the head. "*Allez.*"

He was already seated on the sofa and studying with his rapid and precise glance the antique paintings on the walls, illuminated by the flames of the great candles lit in the sitting-room and therefore appearing even gloomier than they would by daylight, when Anna Sergeyevna entered, still in her very low-cut ballgown. The light of the candles ran and flowed over her shoulders and bosom. She sat down in an armchair opposite her guest and said confidingly:

"And I took you for an adventurer. But you are an adventurer in whom I can find at least one virtue: you are not like the others."

Now that he had removed his fur coat, his emaciation was obvious; but his beauty only gained from this. For a moment Anna Sergeyevna wondered if he really were a living man, whether the astonishing perfection of that face would have been better suited to a statue or a painting.

"I think you are not very far off the truth," said her guest. "I am, if you will, an adventurer. But I am not an evildoer, in any case."

"Oh, you need not have said that," said Anna Sergeyevna, smiling. "No evildoer could have such a face. You are very good, I am sure. And yet there is something about you I don't like," she added, with a kind of defenseless candor.

He took her hands; and this touch alone, radiating imperceptibly swiftly across Anna Sergeyevna's skin, immediately forced her to realize the inexplicable power the adventurer had over her. Her face even changed a little, twisting for a second into an uncharacteristic grimace.

"What splendidly alert responses," the adventurer said slowly, as if speaking to himself. "How excellent. Do you have pure Russian blood in your veins?" he asked. "That would surprise me very much. I see some kind of dark streak. Are all your family Russians?"

"No," replied Anna Sergeyevna, surprised, "no, in fact. My grandfather was the son of a Norwegian and an Italian woman."

"That is the dullest kind of union," said the guest. "The Norwegians are the most stupefying of all. But you have always lived in Russia?"

"Always."

"I once saw a woman, very like you – but that was a few years ago. She was an Irishwoman. Do you like Ireland?"

"I have never been to Ireland."

"Perhaps, then, you like England?"

"I have never been to England."

"But surely there's no need to live in a country to like it or dislike it. I can assure you that I loved the Philippines, and also San Francisco, and London before I succeeded in going to any of them. And I love Paris very much, though I have never seen it."

"What? Are you really not a Frenchman?"

"No," her guest answered with a smile. "I am not a Frenchman. I am an American."

"An American?" repeated Anna Sergeyevna in surprise. "That doesn't seem like you at all. What is your given name?"

The adventurer did not reply immediately.

"My name is Edgar," he said. "Edgar Allan Poe."

"You don't look like a man of business," said Anna Sergeyevna. "And even less like a colonist."

"I am neither a businessman nor a trader. I am – please don't be frightened – a poet."

"Whatever are you doing here, in Russia?"

"You have already forgotten that I am an adventurer," said Edgar, with a smile. "An adventurer goes everywhere; that makes him an adventurer. I have no very clear idea of why I came to Russia. But, in any case, I will sincerely regret that within a few hours I must leave your country and I will never be able to speak with you again."

"Do you write poems? There is nothing for you to do in Russia, we have no poetry. The French are better."

"Not in my experience," said Edgar. "The French, in my view, are bad poets."

"What! What about Corneille? And Racine? And Ronsard? Or Boileau?"

"Of them all only Ronsard is anything like a poet. The others are not poets; that's a misconception. They are either imitators, or office clerks. Incidentally, I don't like Ronsard either."

"Then whom do you like?"

"François Villon," said Edgar swiftly. "And Alain Chartier. He was, perhaps, an unsuccessful poet, but a wonderful man."

"I have always envied poets," remarked Anna Sergeyevna. But, glancing at her companion, she saw that his beautiful face had darkened and frowned, that his eyes had squinted and dimmed and that his lips were twitching rapidly and horribly; she felt afraid despite herself, remembering how at first sight she had noticed something insane about his face.

"May God," Edgar spoke, slowly, "may God have mercy upon you, if you ever find yourself in the power of phantoms, or wings, or implacable eyes. And of that face," he spoke as if delirious, "from which you can never escape. And of that knowledge, which forces you to note the awkwardness of a mother's shudders beside the corpse of her son, the comical jerks of a dying body, or the slightly lopsided bosom of the woman who has in that very moment become the mother of my child."

He fell silent, then began again with the same plaintive intonation which had sounded in his voice when he had complained of the cold.

"May I be allowed to die peacefully. I can't last any longer. I can never rest – and for many years already, everything revolves before my sight, and disappears, and appears again – people, objects, countries; at night I dream and in my dreams I see my corpse lying on the ground."[1]

She was silent, not knowing what to say to this strange man.

"And then," he went on, "I know too many things and I feel too much, too deeply. I see through opaque surfaces; I hear the notes of the violin inside its case and the chime of unmoving bells. Do you find this strange?"

"Yes. But are you sure that you always see and hear the things of which you speak?"

"Always," he answered, despairingly. "Give me your hand."

Anna Sergeyevna stretched out her hand to him. Her fingers were trembling. Edgar's hand was cold and steady, and this time she did not shudder at his touch. But the longer her hot little fingers held Edgar's hand, the warmer and more alive the adventurer's hand became. His dull eyes, looking off to one side, gradually came to life.

"I will tell you just one thing, to prove that I am neither fantasizing nor mistaken," said Edgar. "I see that you have a white scar on your left breast almost right over your heart, a touch below it. Where did you get that?"

Anna Sergeyevna, knowing that Edgar could not see the scar, shivered.

"I got that scar," she said in a hushed voice, turning pale again, "when as a little girl I wounded myself, stumbling on the veranda and falling against a sharp iron scraper, the kind we use for cleaning snow or dirt off our boots. But can you really see it?"

"I can see it," said Edgar, mournfully. "I see another thing also: you will soon have a child."

"That can't be true," said Anna Sergeyevna, blushing like a girl.

"My dear," said the adventurer in a different voice, which Anna Sergeyevna felt as if she had known forever, "don't misunderstand

---

1. Gazdanov is adapting a line from Edgar Allan Poe's 1844 short story, "A Tale of the Ragged Mountains": "Beneath me lay my corpse, with the arrow in my temple." He will cite it again (and make it a major plot motif) of his novel *The Specter of Alexander Wolf* (1947).

me. I know that you are living alone now. No, I am not saying what you thought at first, or for the reason you suspected. But everything that will happen already exists, even before it takes place in reality. So the birth of your child already exists in this room; and I also see this because the blood in your veins is too thick and too hot. My death exists here now; and in this small space, which you and I see around us, there is an entire town in America or England, where I will die. Let's say, rather, in America, since it's far away from us. Why aren't you astonished by memory? Memory is vision turned backwards. But there are some whom God has allowed to see their own lives in advance. Imagine you are standing somewhere far away, at the edge of a long pathway, lit by a torch. A fiery banner is approaching you: it lights up along the path the towns where you will live, the faces of the people you will see, the bodies of the women whom you will love. Then in the final moment it lights up the black ocean into which you will be plunged forever; the red flame scorches your face and breast, and you die."

He stopped. The candles in the sitting-room were guttering; trembling shadows rushed across the ceiling; outside the window it was cold and dark. Anna Sergeyevna recalled how as a little girl, lying in bed, she would toss and turn under her blanket, pulling it over her head to pretend this was her cave, or a big nest, or a den, where no one could reach her and where her little body would be warm and comfortable. This feeling, changing with the years, had never quite left her; it was especially strong in autumnal weather with cold rain or a snowstorm, when Anna Sergeyevna sat before blazing logs, feeling remote from all misfortunes and sorrows, in warmth and peace. At this moment, sitting opposite the silent Edgar, she felt a sudden chill, as if the room, so safe until then, had been entered by the cold stones of foreign cities, the icy breath of the frozen land; and as if here, beside her, lay a stiff body with a dead and beautiful face.

"How strange," she said, "how strange all this is. I never thought that such a man might exist in the world. Even in America. Why are you this way?" she asked. "Don't be surprised by my naiveté. I can't find any other words now."

"I don't know why," said Edgar. "I know that in the eyes of all those who know me I am merely a tramp and a madman. I studied in England, became a soldier, I know several languages, I am strong and healthy – and it seems to me there is nothing I don't understand. When strangers speak to me, I know what they are about to say; I can always tell whether a passerby will die a violent death or expire in his own home; I recognize a card-sharper even before he picks up his cards; and I know a thief passing at the other end of the street. I know how and why the woman with whom I speak will love me, and why she will weep later on. I hear the echoes of snow and of words not yet uttered, but which people are about to pronounce; I can guess with my eyes closed whether there will be a man or a woman in a house I am entering for the first time; I can sense how a war no one has even thought of yet flies through the air like a heavy cloud; and, while I sit in my chair in London, I hear the cracking and splintering of a boat just then sinking to the deeps in the middle of the Pacific Ocean. But I do not know why I am doomed to these torments nor what dreadful law ordains that I must live surrounded by a dozen deaths every day."

Recalling this conversation and what happened afterwards, Anna Sergeyevna always felt sorrow; her chest would tighten, as if someone near and dear to her were in deadly danger. She walked over to the adventurer, sat beside him and started to stroke his hair.

"Poor Edgar," she murmured, "poor Edgar!"

He did not make the slightest movement. His head lay on her warm shoulder.

From a distant room a cuckoo-clock called, and then all became peaceful again. Edgar's head never moved, his eyes were closed; but she could picture, although she could not see, an alert and wary shadow on the wall behind them; and so she knew he was not sleeping.

Before Edgar's closed eyes a wide, peaceful river was flowing. The voices of far-off strangers called to each other across it; the swift rushing of the waters and the bubbling of playful fish complemented these cries. The river flowed on, and grew wider, and altered color; now it skirted yellow banks with far-off, barely visible little hovels, becoming turbid and gray; then it turned bluer, like molten steel, passing a low castle, encircled by trees. "This is the Rhine," thought Edgar.

And there, in the distance, where the river merged with the sea, in the cold seaside fog rose a gigantic figure, holding in its hand a burning torch. The river drew closer to it; and before Edgar's eyes a broad patch of sky was illuminated, where black broken masts and ripped sails swayed desperately; and, inexplicably clinging to the air without tumbling downwards, phantoms were thronging and wings were beating; and on these waves of air a face was rocking steadily, as if dozing, but dreadfully alive. This face had long haunted Edgar and slowly followed him – on ships and carriages, through England, Scotland, and Russia; for it, as for himself, neither death, nor danger, nor distance existed.

"I am not yours yet," Edgar said slowly and furiously in English. "I am not yours yet."

And then he became aware of the hand that had never ceased stroking him. He took it and kissed it, then placed it back upon his hair, dropping his head, and Anna Sergeyevna imagined that he had fallen asleep. She looked into his face. He was sleeping peacefully, his breast rising and falling evenly; his long eyelashes threw a shadow on his white, still face; and only on the left corner of his lips, a tiny bubble of rose-pink foam had not yet burst.

1930

THE WATCH

Yevgeny Zamyatin

No lately departed great folk will take the stage in this tale. My humble hero Semyon Zaitser – or, if you prefer, Comrade Zaitser – flourishes to the present day, living at the very same address, No. 7 Caravan Street in Leningrad. Yet this tale is no less historical for all that; the events to be described took place in that romantic era when time in Russia was still counted in years, and not in Five-Year Plans; when vodka was proclaimed a bourgeois poison and seekers after oblivion drank *eau de cologne*; when gunshots crackled all night in the blue, frosty wilderness of the Petersburg streets; when jolly footpads released passers-by to scurry home in nothing but their collar and tie; when the best possible present for one's beloved was a pound of sugar tied up with a ribbon; and when Comrade Zaitser acquired his celebrated gold watch all for a single cartload of firewood.

Zaitser was a mighty individual; he was in charge of procuring firewood for the whole of freezing Petersburg; he signed requisitions for logs, he made people warm, and, like the sun, he was round, rubicund, and radiant. And if you have ever had the temerity to stare at the sun, you have probably noticed that its expression is not only radiant, but even slightly astonished by its own radiance. This very same expression of astonishment at himself was on Comrade Zaitser's face; his brows were always arched expressively upwards, as if he still could not believe that he, Zaitser, only yesterday a tailor's apprentice in the town of Pinsk, now sat in his very own office, with his secretary

Verochka at his disposal, with a gold watch in his waistcoat pocket, and...

However, perhaps we should show all our cards at once and, without squandering precious lines, let us state plainly that the above-mentioned pound of sugar tied up with a pink ribbon had been obtained by none other than Comrade Zaitser for his secretary Verochka, and that he had acquired the gold watch also for Verochka's sake – as a kind of antidote to the silver Caucasian belt which had appeared the day before yesterday on the slender waist of Comrade Kubas, the secretary for the Communist cell and editor of the wall newspaper[1] in Zaitser's department.

But Verochka – alas! – had not noticed the celebrated gold watch. Comrade Zaitser had already fiddled with the lid several times; he had placed the watch in front of him on a pile of papers; and yet Verochka continued to stare vaguely out of the window at the drifting snowflakes. Comrade Zaitser could restrain himself no longer; he said:

"Listen, Comrade Verochka, have you ever seen a watch like this, eh? Let me tell you – you've never seen a better one!"

He whirled the watch in the air, thrust it into his waistcoat pocket, and at that very moment Verochka heard, as if rising from the depths of Zaitser himself, the tenderest fairy music followed by a silvery peal: nine o'clock. Verochka opened her eyes wide (they were sea-blue). Zaitser, beaming, explained that all you had to do was imperceptibly press the watch "just here, on its, as you might say, tummy – and there you have both the music and the time!" Immediately Verochka wanted to try for herself – might she? Heavens above, what sort of question was that! Well, of course she might!

Verochka stepped towards Comrade Zaitser. Her hand felt about for the music hidden on his breast (more precisely – in his waistcoat pocket). Her neck and her arm, bare to the elbow, came very close

---

1. A wall newspaper was a hand-printed, publicly displayed propaganda sheet, produced by workers in the Soviet Union for the information of all staff in their factory or organization.

indeed before Zaitser's eyes. Verochka was almost gilded; her skin had a delicate golden down all over, as if she were lightly furred: and perhaps this was the very quality about her that could drive any man out of his wits. When Verochka finally found the watch and pressed it with her hand, she might well have been gently squeezing Comrade Zaitser's heart instead. His captured heart beat faster, and he made up his mind; as soon as the watch finished playing its tune, he would instantly tell Verochka what he had long yearned to tell her without ever gathering the courage.

Very likely he would have told her, if Comrade Kubas had not entered the office at that very moment. Verochka, blushing red, straightened up, Zaitser shuffled his papers, and a smile like the tail of a venomous snake flickered and vanished in the corner of Comrade Kubas's lips. He deliberately paused for a moment before announcing, in a drily official tone, that Comrade Vera had to be seconded that day for the production of the current edition of the wall newspaper. Zaitser smiled welcomingly: "My dear Comrade Kubas, you must have forgotten, that this evening we have a meeting and I must dictate a report to *my*," he stressed the word, "secretary about the spring campaign for procuring firewood. Comrade Vera, please fetch your typewriter in here, if you would…"

Verochka departed. As she lifted the dust cover off the typewriter, she heard through the office door the voices inside becoming ever louder, rising to yells. "Without her, I can't issue the wall newspaper! You'll disrupt my work for the political education of the labor force!" Kubas was shouting. "And you're sticking a spoke in the wheel of heating the Red capital!" Zaitser bawled back. Verochka realized that the political education of the workers and the heating of the Red capital each depended upon her. But her heart still hesitated to choose: would it be Comrade Zaitser or Comrade Kubas? Zaitser was warm and cozy; he had firewood and a watch and an apartment (not just a room, but a whole apartment!). Kubas had that slender waist encircled by a silver belt; his eyes were sharp and birdlike; he scared her a little, but…

What this "but" meant, Verochka wasn't sure. She was sure of one thing only: the time had come. If not now, in the office, then that evening, that night, or tomorrow morning, everything must be settled at last. But how? How could she avoid making a mistake she would later regret? Verochka sighed, cautiously lifted the heavy machine – as heavy as her destiny – in her downy arms and carried it towards the fateful decision in the office.

"Be seated, please," Zaitser said to Verochka. "I'll start dictating to you right away."

"Aha, is that how it is? Very well then!" Comrade Kubas stabbed Zaitser with a glance, and departed.

Verochka placed her hands upon the keyboard. In the silence, she could hear how heavily Zaitser was breathing. He stared at her hands… Outside the window, the downy snow was falling.

"Yes… Well, then, spring it is," said Zaitser.

"Spring?" Verochka was startled.

"If I say it's spring, then it's spring! Write: 'As the start of our spring campaign approaches…'"

In spite of the weather, Comrade Zaitser was right. Do you imagine spring is all rose-pink tints, blue skies and nightingales? Mere sentimental prejudice! On a snowy meadow, two stags which were grazing side by side just the day before now hurl themselves on one another for the sake of a lady deer – that's spring for you. People who yesterday were as peaceful as deer, today turn into heroes and paint the snow with their blood – that's spring for you. The color of spring is not blue, not rose-pink, but red – the red of danger, passion, frenzy, battle.

The evening meeting in Zaitser's office was one such battle; more precisely, a duel. Verochka feverishly typed up the pistol shots – there was no other word for the remarks exchanged by the combatants. Kubas peppered every point in Zaitser's report with twenty-two citations from Lenin. Every cord of wood was contested like the famous Ferryman's House in the battles of the Marne.[2]

"Listen, Comrade Kubas, we won't be finished before morning if we keep this up!" the chairman burst out.

To avoid being compromised by the capitalist glitter of gold, Zaitser had placed his watch in his desk drawer before the meeting began. Now he subtly opened the drawer and glanced inside: midnight. By the time they cast their ballots, the bells of the last trams had already fallen silent, and nocturnal robbers were already on the hunt. Verochka feverishly counted the votes: she knew that the real matter at issue was not cubic meters of firewood, but human hearts.

Ten votes to one. That one, utterly defeated, cinched his silver Caucasian belt more tightly and left, without a word of farewell to anyone. And, naturally, as the happy victor, Zaitser set off to walk Verochka home.

The ravine-like streets, shining faintly with snow, were dark and empty; there wasn't a soul anywhere, not even a glimmer of lamplight in the dark windows. Had Comrade Zaitser been alone now in this wilderness, perhaps he would have crept along on tip-toe, so that no one would hear the scrape of his shoes on the snow; and very probably he would have leapt aside from the first passerby he met, and indeed fled into the distance at full speed. But now, when a shot rang out somewhere ahead and Verochka's warm arm trembled against his, Zaitser merely chuckled:

"Now what's the matter? Let them take pot shots at each other; I'm by your side."

This was a new and heroic Zaitser. This Zaitser even wanted something terrifying to happen; he feared nothing. Except just one thing: the conversation he was about to have with Verochka. Good

---

2. Zamyatin has confused locations here. The Ferryman's House, or Maison du Passeur, was a strategically key building near a bridge over the River Yser in Belgium (not the Marne, in France). In October 1914, the Ferryman's House became briefly famous when a French colonial regiment, armed only with bayonets, recaptured it from German forces equipped with machine guns.

heavens – where to begin? The beginning was the most fearsome part of all.

Zaitser savagely rotated the top button on his coat, as if it was preventing him from opening his mouth. The button finally popped off. Zaitser began to speak:

"I want to tell you, Verochka, a certain thing…"

"Here it comes!" Verochka's arm trembled again, just as it had a little while ago when they heard the shot.

"What sort of thing?" Verochka enquired, although she already knew very well.

"My mother's cat had kittens yesterday!" Zaitser blurted.

Verochka stared at Zaitser in utter bafflement. Screwing up his eyes, he continued in a warm and tender tone:

"You know, she just lies there and croons to herself, with her seven little kittens around her! And I look at them and tell myself, 'Oh, Semyon, you could croon like that too, like that fortunate cat with her little family…'"

Evidently, Verochka had rather too vividly imagined Comrade Zaitser in the position of the fortunate cat: a little dimple on her right cheek was quivering, and she covered her mouth with a hand. Zaitser saw this and understood: she was about to start laughing out loud, and then all would be ruined… He waited in horror for her laughter, just as in Tolstoy's novels the heroes wait for a spinning bomb to explode.

But suddenly he felt Verochka's fingers tightly squeeze his arm; her whole body pressed against his. Zaitser wanted to yell with the ferocity of his joy. He bent closer to Verochka…

"Just *look*!" Verochka whispered fearfully to him.

And then Zaitser saw: a tall man in a military greatcoat with no insignia was walking swiftly across the street, to cut them off. For a single second, no more, the old Zaitser reappeared, creeping backwards. But almost instantly the new, heroic Zaitser commanded Verochka, "Hide in the entryway!" strode towards the bandit and, occupying a spot not far from the dark doorway that had swallowed up Verochka, he halted. Zaitser was shaking all over, but not with fear: this was how a seething boiler shudders when pressurized beyond its fifteen-atmosphere limit.

The man in the military greatcoat walked up to him and also halted. There was a dreadful, endless pause. Zaitser could wait no longer. Huskily, he said:

"Well, what is it?"

Keeping his hand in his pocket (did he have a revolver?), the man remained silent. Zaitser managed to glimpse his impudent whiskers, like Kaiser Wilhelm's, and his very white, strong teeth.

The man's silence was obviously a mockery: that much was clear to Zaitser. And it grew even clearer when the whiskers finally twitched to ask thickly:

"Got any matches?"

Zaitser was boiling over; he longed to hurl himself at the man that instant, land a blow; but he rose to the challenge, he pretended to believe the request for matches. He took out his box and struck one. The man leaned right into Zaitser, unceremoniously grabbing his lapel and stretching it to shelter the match-flame from the wind, and lit up. Zaitser saw a ring sparkling on the man's finger (snatched from somebody else that very night, perhaps). Zaitser felt the light, barely noticeable touch of a hand. He had an urge to blow out the match, if only so as not to see those mockingly twitching whiskers, when suddenly, in the red glare of the little flame, before Zaitser's eyes, a gold watch floated through the air.

A certain quotient of seconds was required for Zaitser to grasp just how the robber had pulled off the trick with the cigarette. And still more seconds went by before he clutched at his waistcoat pocket, where his watch no longer lay. Zaitser's heart thumped furiously, and he hurled the still-burning match directly into the robber's face, snatched his watch from him and roared savagely (he had never suspected that he was capable of using such a voice):

"Hands up! I'll shoot!" And he plunged his hand into his own coat pocket.

This action was so decisive, and his counterattack was so unexpected, that the robber did raise his hands; but then, without waiting for Zaitser to shoot, he crouched, turned about, and dashed off into the darkness beyond.

Zaitser drew his handkerchief out of his coat pocket (naturally, he had never had any revolver there) and wiped away his perspiration. He was still trembling all over when a pale Verochka rushed up to him.

"What happened? What happened?" she seized his arm.

"Nothing happened. Well…" Zaitser waved the regained watch in his hand. "What a scoundrel! He'd managed to grab this, can you imagine? But he made a serious mistake when he decided to take me on."

"But how could you not be afraid, that he… No, I never dreamed, that you were – that kind of man!" Verochka's eyes shone ecstatically.

"I'll tell you this, Verochka, that even if he had fired at me, it would have made no difference, because at this moment I feel like a madman, because I… you… Oh dear God, Verochka, you know very well why!"

Verochka, with shining eyes, said nothing. But there, underneath, in the darkness, Verochka's hand, gently, like a little cat, slowly crept into Zaitser's sleeve. His palms brushed the unbearably soft down of her wrist. Zaitser's heart broke loose, like a sweet, ripe apple falling from a branch.

"Well, why aren't you saying anything? I can't stand this anymore!" Zaitser shouted.

"I would rather tell you in the morning, if you don't mind."

But Verochka's eyes and the gentle movement of her hand had already told Zaitser everything… All that was left for the morning, seemingly, was a banal happy ending. However, it might be more correct to say that only those envious folk whom fate prevents from feeling the joys of spring (regardless of the season of the year) would ever call a happy ending banal.

It is not known whether Comrade Zaitser slept at all on that snowy spring night (it is unlikely). It is not known whether Verochka slept (perhaps she did). But the next morning, before Comrade Zaitser arrived, everyone in his department already knew that he was a hero. When he finally appeared, he was surrounded, showered with questions, congratulations, and smiles. Without stopping, muttering something indistinct, Zaitser hurried into his office. Strange to say, his expression failed utterly to correspond with his heroic position: he was pale and distracted. Perhaps this was the result of a sleepless night; perhaps he was too agitated about the expected encounter with Verochka and her promised reply. Even more strangely, after running into his office, he merely shot Verochka a frightened, sideways glance, nodded to her, and immediately rushed over to his desk. Hurriedly unbuttoning his jacket, he drew out his gold watch, threw it on a pile of papers, pulled out the desk drawer, and, bending over it, froze. His eyebrows rose to the highest level nature would allow.

"What's happened?" Verochka ran fearfully over to him.

"What's happened?" Zaitser said in an unfamiliar voice. "Look what's happened!"

From his desk drawer, he removed and laid down beside his gold watch... another gold watch. Verochka watched round-eyed, understanding nothing.

"So it was I who robbed *him* – that scoundrel!" screeched Zaitser, in despair. "This is *my* watch, it was lying here in its place, but that wretched robber had his own watch – now do you understand?"

Verochka understood. Zaitser watched the little dimple on her right cheek tremble. She turned aside. There was a strange sound, resembling a strangled sob; a second later, spasms of frenzied, uncontrollable laughter; and Verochka flew headlong through the door.

More than likely she collapsed there, shuddering and gasping, on the first chair she found. From inside the office she could be heard telling, or more precisely, yelling, something to the co-workers crowding around her. And after that, a guffaw like a landslide, sweeping from room to room and floor to floor, filled Comrade Zaitser's entire department.

Thrusting his fingers into his hair, he sat alone in his office. The two gold watches lay before him. When the door creaked and someone poked their head inside the office, Zaitser muttered without raising his eyes:

"I'm busy now. Tomorrow…"

No one dared to try to see him after that; Verochka least of all. She knew that as soon as she saw him she would lose control and once again laugh in his face.

When the sound of the last footsteps had faded from the department, when the last doors had slammed, Zaitser stood up, slipped into his pocket his own (really his own) watch, and walked over to the little table where Verochka's typewriter stood under its dust cover. He gazed bitterly on her empty chair, hands pressed to his heart. Next to his heart lay the watch – and that cursed watch, which had doomed him, began to play its tune. Furiously, Zaitser crushed it with his fist to stop the music. Something crunched inside the watch; it fell silent.

Through the empty, unpeopled rooms, the staircase, the entrance hall he went. On the wall of the entrance hall, Zaitser saw the special edition of the wall newspaper, which Kubas had released that day (perhaps with Verochka's assistance). It featured a cartoon of a funny little man with ferociously arched brows, holding an enormous watch in each hand. Underneath was a caption in bold type: "Hands up!"

Zaitser hastily turned away and walked, forever, out of his department, out of Verochka's heart, and out of this story.

1934

THE ENCOUNTER

Yevgeny Zamyatin

A man with a bristly crew-cut, wearing the uniform of a tsarist secret-police colonel, rapped out his report in a military manner, and sat down. He had carried out the search of the accused man's dwelling, and his testimony was incontestable, accurate, and damning. But the accused was not even looking at him. Barely breathing, afraid to stir, he was listening to the regular tread of soldiers' feet: at any moment the prison convoy was sure to enter the room, and with them, his last hope of rescue. The accused knew that the convoy was commanded by Popov, a fellow revolutionary, and that Popov would attempt to pass him a revolver at the right moment.

But Popov came only as far as the dais where the judges were seated; here, instead of marching his convoy up to the accused, he stopped in distraction. Unblinking, craning his neck, he stared into the far corner of the room. His neck was unusually slender for his wide shoulders – as if it had been taken in error from another man's torso. He stood gazing in astonishment at the police colonel, forgetting everything else.

Apart from the colonel, no one noticed; no one knew the reason for his bewilderment. Indeed, even the colonel didn't understand the reason; he merely sensed the unblinking gaze of the convoy officer with the giraffe-like neck become fixed on him.

The bell rang earlier than expected: break-time. The rest of the court session was put off. The judges, glittering with generals' epaulettes, rose and bustled about. They all hurried to the canteen, hoping to have time to gulp down a cup of tea or coffee there. The last to leave the room were an immense, red-faced cabby and a bald tramp, who had also been summoned to act as witnesses in the trial.

The canteen seemed dark after the brightly lit courtroom – the lusterless, dusty lamps were additionally veiled by tobacco fumes. The draft from an open window made the door slam every time it was opened, and set the ceiling lamps swaying lightly – and everything underneath also swayed lightly; everything was unsteady, as if in a dream. And, indeed, especially after the stark reality of what had transpired in the courtroom, everything here did resemble a dream or a hallucination.

Soldiers, gypsies, peasants, and officers flickered by in the smoky gloom. The priest who had been swearing in witnesses embraced a gypsy and burst into a popular ditty. The police colonel amiably seated himself at the little table where the cabby and the tramp were quarrelling over something. "Your Excellency, why are you allowing yourself to get so excited?" he inquired of the tramp. Here, in this dream, no one was surprised that the tramp assumed the title of "Excellency" as his due, but even so the colonel still found it rather awkward when the tramp pointed crossly at the cabby: "Because Ensign Simkov has permitted himself to sit at my table, without first asking my permission, as required by regulations. He forgets my rank!" The ensign-cum-cabby, his belly wobbling good-naturedly, guffawed: "Here we are all the same rank, my dear fellow! Bit players! And we all have the same price: a hundred francs a day. The colonel is the exception: firstly, because he gets a hundred and twenty, secondly, because he plays himself. That's called 'striking it lucky'!"

And truly, he had struck it lucky: in this film from Russian life, the former secret police colonel had been given the role of a secret police colonel. The director said he acted magnificently, but he never acted at all: he simply became what he had been before. He became himself to such a degree, down to such tiny details, that now, as he finished his cigarette, he struck a light with exactly the same lazy movement as in the old days – and, just as he had then, he tossed away the still-burning match.

From above, through the fog of tobacco-smoke, a hand emerged and took the match from the ashtray as it smoldered. The colonel glanced up – and met the gaze of the long-necked convoy officer, Popov. Bending down, Popov stared the colonel straight in the face. The match burnt down and singed his fingers; he tossed it aside without lighting up, then silently disappeared in the phantasmagorical crowd of gypsies, soldiers, and peasants.

"What can this mean?" said the colonel. "What can what mean?" the cabby asked in surprise. The colonel tried to explain, but failed, because in truth, nothing had happened. More precisely, only one thing had happened: the colonel was sure that he had seen this long-necked officer somewhere before. But when? Where? In Crimea? In Constantinople? He just could not recall, and the thought gave him no peace, like a fish bone lodged somewhere in one's teeth that absolutely must be pulled out.

The ensign-cabby, chuckling lusciously, was telling a story about a gypsy and a garter, but his words never reached the colonel: the fish bone blocked them. Or perhaps that wasn't the trouble: he simply wanted to drink, but they still hadn't brought his coffee. The waiter flew through the fog again near their table. The colonel swung around to catch him – and sitting behind, very near, he saw Popov again: right before the priest's nose, he was dandling two revolvers in his hands. "Why the hell do you bring a real gun around with you, when they give you a fake one here?" the priest asked. "I ah-adore revolvers... ever since my childhood..." said Popov, stammering slightly.

As soon as the colonel heard this gulping, stammering voice inside his head, just as in a theater, the curtains instantly parted – and he remembered everything, even saw it with a clarity that frightened him.

This man, then in a student's uniform, had been sitting with his back to him, hunched over an iron table in a prison cell. The colonel was watching him through a glass spyhole in the door. The student was absorbed in what he was doing and noticed nothing: in front of him on the tiny table were chessmen fashioned out of bread; he was playing against himself. The colonel entered the room, grabbed the crosshatched sheet of paper together with the chess pieces, balled them up and shoved them into his pocket. He was a chess-player himself and thus he knew that this would be the most painful punishment for the prisoner, and this stubborn boy deserved punishment. The student glanced at the colonel and said nothing, merely gulped visibly, his Adam's apple sliding up and down his slender neck. The colonel, without taking his eyes from the boy's neck, told him very gently: "You will be allowed a meeting with your fiancée. I explained to her that if you remain silent, you will face the noose, and she has promised to persuade you to be more forthcoming."

The student had not one, but several meetings with his fiancée. This situation wore on for a whole month. The colonel heard the girl weeping, pleading, kissing him. In the end the student had told all. When the colonel signed off the order for his release, the student stared at him for a second, unblinking, with hate-filled eyes, then said, stammering: "It w-would have been b-b-better if you'd hanged me! And you sh-should kn-know, if w-we meet again s-sometime…" He faltered and, never finishing his phrase, walked out.

And now, here, they met again. Around them in the delirious fog flickered pretend gypsies, officers, peasants, and beggars. Only the two of them were playing their original roles: the colonel – as himself, Popov – as a revolutionary, although he now wore an officer's uniform. And then a bell rang in the canteen, summoning them to continue the play – and, perhaps, to bring it to an end.

The ensign-cabby and the indigent Excellency had left before the bell. The colonel made his way alone to the studio. That student would not leave his head. The colonel remembered that the fiancée had been called Musya and that once he had seen how she, blushing, had tried to hide her finger, which was showing through a rip in her glove; but he had completely forgotten her face. "What a strange thing memory is! You can forget a person's face – and recall a torn glove," thought the colonel.

He opened a door – and found himself in a semi-dark courtyard, piled with enormous empty boxes. He realized he had forgotten to turn right when he should have, and now he could not figure out which way to go. Feeling with his hands, he finally found the door by which he had entered, pulled it open – and stopped. Before him stood the so-called "Popov." Stretching his long neck, grinning unpleasantly, he said, "L-l-lost your way?" And he carried on standing there, watching the colonel and keeping his hands in his pockets.

"Any moment now he'll take a pistol out of his pocket," thought the colonel, feeling the hair stand up on his head. He felt angry at himself and stepped decisively towards Popov: "Allow me to pass!" Popov, without taking his hands from his pockets, moved aside. The colonel walked on, hearing steps behind him, ever closer. With all his strength, he strove not to hurry – but he could feel himself walking faster all the time.

He ran into the studio, panting for breath. They were waiting for him. The director, loudly and in front of everyone, reproached him for lateness, but the colonel could only think of one thing: more than likely, he – this Popov – was also listening…

The colonel glanced around: Popov was sitting on his right, a little behind, so that the colonel had only to turn slightly to see those unblinking, unflinching eyes. Then, without turning, he somehow felt that gaze on the back of his head, on his neck, on his right ear (which was burning) – binding and enmeshing him, like a spider's web.

The director shouted, "Allons!" and the lamps hissed. The colonel stood up, to once again repeat his ten words, condemning the prisoner. He wished, as his former self had done, to extend a hand, pointing out the prisoner; but sideways, from the corner of his eye, he could see that Popov had also risen, keeping his hands in his pockets. The colonel made some entirely clumsy, wooden motion with his hand and fell silent mid-sentence: all the words had suddenly flown out of his head. "What's the matter with you, man? Did you drink too much, or are you sick?" the director yelled at him. "Get out of here – come back when you've had a breath of air..."

Someone sniggered. Hunched over, trying to look smaller, less noticeable, the colonel left the studio. However, he was no longer a colonel, not the man he'd been these last days; once again, he was that man who not long ago had been washing windows for loose change. He walked down the long, white, empty corridor and, squeezing his hands into fists, told the director in his thoughts everything that he would have told him aloud, if he could.

The canteen was empty of people and, for the sake of economy, only one lamp was lit. The colonel sat at a table, ordered coffee, then stopped the waiter: "No, better give me some cognac!" The waiter asked him something. "It doesn't matter what kind – just be quick about it!" the colonel waved his hand crossly: simmering, he continued to express his feelings to the director, and to this waiter as well...

But suddenly he forgot the director, and his wounded feelings, and the waiter, and everything else: Popov was coming through the doors and over to his table, his head bobbing on his slender neck. He stopped in front of the colonel and, as if still making up his mind, groped for something in his pocket. The colonel already knew what that "something" must be. His heart started knocking at his ribs, but his hands and feet were bound as if by a web, and he could neither rise nor cry out.

The waiter brought coffee and cognac, placed them on the table and went into the kitchen. The former colonel and the former student were left together. The colonel listened to the sound of a large fly buzzing and blundering against the ceiling.

"And to think I knew you s-straightaway," said "Popov," once again rooting around in his pocket.

The colonel wanted to say, "What do you want from me?" but he knew the words would come out clumsily, comically; he knew, after all, why this man had found him here. He waited unmoving; only his heart was thumping, even harder.

"D-do you remember how in the c-cell you took away my chess pieces? And you t-told me that you were a chess player t-too? I r-remember everything!" went on "Popov," cunningly screwing up his eyes and slowly, gradually withdrawing his hand from his pocket.

The colonel could see nothing now except that hand; it filled up his whole world. He saw how the wrist emerged; he saw a black wristwatch with the dial cracked across. There was still a second to go. The colonel pulled in his head, like a tortoise, and closed his eyes.

One second passed; then two; no shot came. "He's taking aim," the colonel thought suddenly, and, unable to resist, he opened his eyes.

"Popov" was standing in front of him, one hand outstretched, holding a pocket chessboard.

"Shall we play?" he asked and, without waiting for a response, sat down opposite the colonel.

1935

ABOUT THE TRANSLATOR

MUIREANN MAGUIRE is Senior Lecturer in Russian at the University of Exeter, UK. She is a prolific translator whose previous publications include *Red Spectres: Russian Twentieth-Century Gothic-Fantastic Tales* (London: 2012 and New York: 2013), a collection of previously untranslated short stories by Mikhail Bulgakov, Alexander Grin, Sigizmund Krzhizhanovsky and others; and *Before I Croak* (2013), a novel by the Debut Prize-winning author Anna Babiashkina.